MYSTERY
IN THE
BEAR PAW
MOUNTAINS

ISBN: 978-0-9829756-3-3

Published by:
First School Press
P.O. Box 115
Sodus, Michigan 49126

www.firstschoolpress.com

Edited by Rachel Starr Thomson
Cover Design by Jay Cookingham

Note: I would like to thank Dr. Ray Sterner of the Johns Hopkins University Applied Physics Laboratory for his gracious permission in allowing me to use and alter a portion of the 1895 Map of Montana, particularly the old Choteau County, for this book. http://fermi.jhuapl.edu/index.html

Printed in the United States of America

MYSTERY
IN THE
BEAR PAW
MOUNTAINS

MICHAEL LEONARD JEWELL

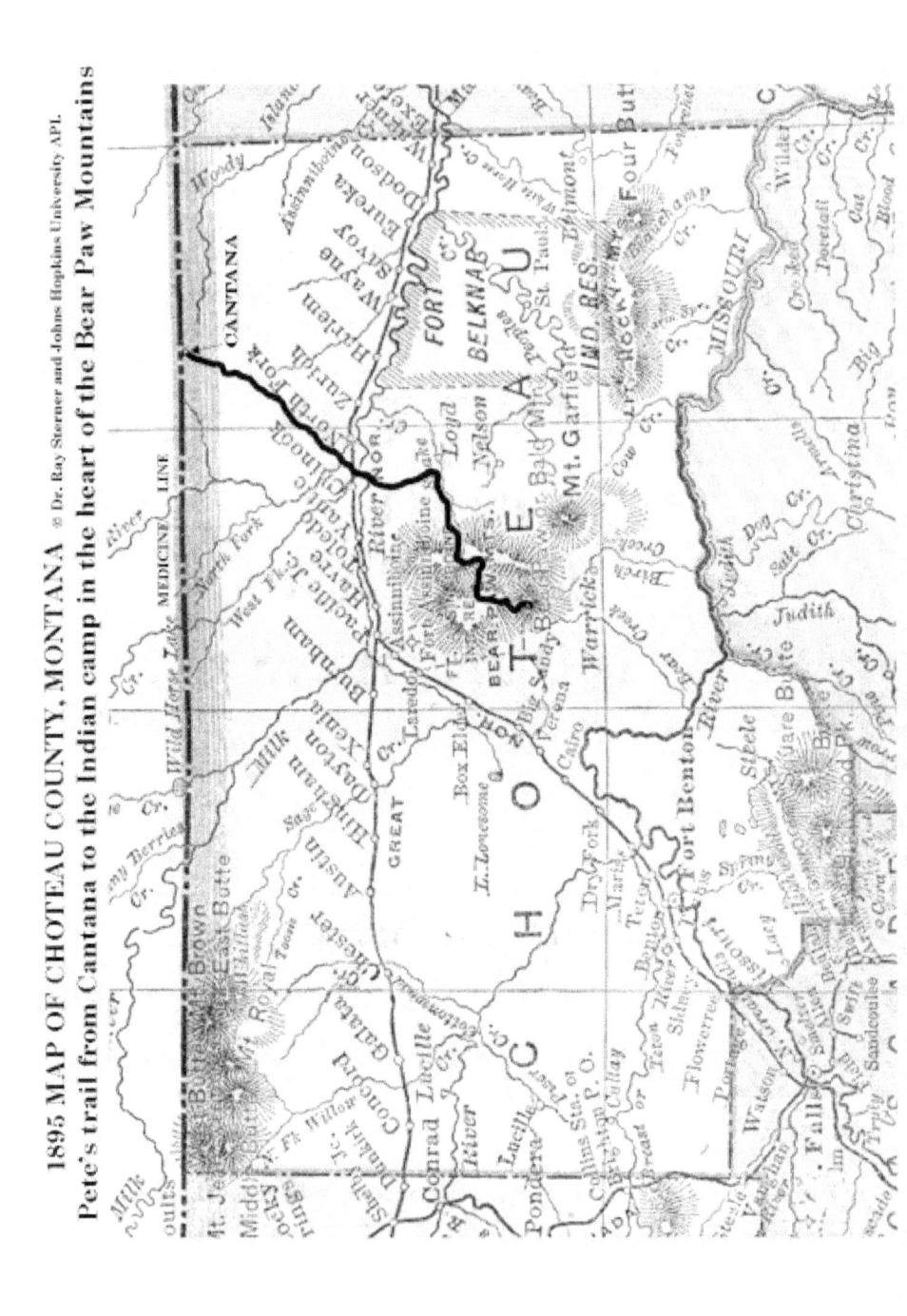

1895 MAP OF CHOTEAU COUNTY, MONTANA © Dr. Ray Sterner and Johns Hopkins University APL.

Pete's trail from Cantana to the Indian camp in the heart of the Bear Paw Mountains

Dedication

To those brave men of color known as Buffalo Soldiers who served with the 10th United States Cavalry.

To the North-West Mounted Police, who broke ground for an amazing law-enforcement tradition represented today by the Royal Canadian Mounted Police.

Finally, to the Nez Perce (Nimíipuu), a great people driven from their home in the Wallowa Valley, Oregon, forced to endure unbelievable hardship, suffering, and humiliation — to the tears of their little ones I dedicate this book.

* * *

To God the Holy Spirit — my ever-present Comforter and Friend.

"And I will pray the Father, and he shall give you another Comforter, that he may abide with you forever."
—John 14:16

Table of Contents

Prologue
CANTANA!

Choteau was once the largest county in the state of Montana. Massive and remote, with over two hundred and fifty miles from its farthest reaches to the county seat at Fort Benton, it was here on this ocean of rolling prairie grass in north-central Montana that the idea for the town of Cantana was born. The name cleverly derived from a contraction of the words *Canada* and *Montana*, this isolated point along the Canadian border was destined to become a city of grand distinction—a San Francisco of the Great Plains!

The plan was to be a simple one. Cantana would attract investors and entrepreneurs speculating on assumptions that the railroad would certainly be built here along the Canadian border. The town of Cantana would then rise from the prairie dust, and when the tracks were finally laid, a handsome profit would be realized from cattlemen transporting cattle to the slaughterhouses in Chicago and mine owners shipping boxcars full of precious ore to the smelters. Returning trains would bring necessities and luxuries to feed the needs and desires of western America and Canada. Visitors from the East—attracted and thrilled by promises of day and night gambling houses, saloons, and other riotous entertainment—would inevitably spend their money by the pocketfuls. Merchants with their wares also hoped to attract locals, handily separating the cow punchers, saddle tramps, bummers, drovers, miners, soldiers, outlaws, drifters, trappers, poachers, and perhaps even Canadians from the few coins that jingled in their pockets. This sticky web of seduction would spin itself out across the plains, with Cantana the fat bejeweled spider poised at its center, ready to pounce upon those who dared come within its reach.

Civilization, however, and unforeseen circumstances and natural disasters, would soon strike Cantana a fatal blow, beginning with Mr. James J. Hill's decision to build the Great Northern Railway further south of the international border. Several dozen one-horse towns quickly sprang up as stops along its east-west corridor, known as the Hi-line. Drought and a series of prairie blizzards all but destroyed the cattle business in the middle eighties, and with the Great Northern built to the south and the Canadian Pacific further to the north, scoffers would claim that the idea of Cantana was doomed from the beginning, carved out on the prairie exactly "betwixt nothin' and nowhere." With acres of empty feedlots and corrals that would never hold cattle, with loading docks and a large train station built along a trackless road, Cantana was like a beautiful debutante all dressed up for a cotillion that was destined never to be. The town and its quick flash of glory seemingly perished overnight, and as the poet Whittier once described the fading of the sun during a snowstorm, "it sank from sight before it set." As Cantana faded in population and importance, it became more isolated. There was presently no working telegraph service, and it would be years before the newfangled telephone would be available in this part of the west. The stagecoach that stopped once every fortnight was the town's only regular communication with the outside world. It brought in the mail, a few supplies, and the odd passenger now and then who looked more lost and bewildered than anything else when he stepped out and looked around. A promised railroad spur had never materialized, so major supplies and desperately needed commodities such as kerosene and coal were hauled in by heavy freight wagons from Harlem, Chinook, and sometimes Havre, always subject to the weather and the sometimes miry and deeply rutted one-track roads.

The few citizens who had remained in Cantana after the boom went bust fully understood that it was only a matter of time before this dubious burg must be abandoned to the inevitable fate of becoming a ghost town. Lonely, deteriorating, neglected, and difficult to resupply, Cantana was going to seed faster than a forgotten bushel of turnips tucked away too long in the corner of a dark, damp root cellar. The low moans of its death rattle could be heard even now, reverberating through its dusty streets, often mistaken for the wind. Only the cemetery at the edge of town could be said to flourish and prosper, never seeming to get its fill of patrons.

And so, Cantana—born of an ambitious dream in the minds of greedy men—was well on its path to being discarded on the ash heap of history with a myriad of other ghost towns in Montana and the Old West.

1
A Brother's Plea

It was November in Cantana, and a succession of heavy frosts and freezes formed a morning's skim of ice on the puddles and horse troughs in town—a warning that a harsh Montana winter was at the very door. Peter Randers, the deputy marshal, stood on the boardwalk in front of the jail watching a brewing storm as it approached from the northwestern sky. Marshal David Brenton was his boss away on business and Pete, awaiting his return, hoped he could avoid what was sure to be the first blast of winter's weather. Slinging the steaming contents of his coffee cup into the street before him, Pete turned and walked back into the jail.

Pete's birth name was really *Peder*, his parents having emigrated from Norway to Minnesota and then Montana Territory. He had been born somewhere east of St. Paul along the Wisconsin border. His father, skilled in trailing, tracking, and all manner of woodman's lore from his days in the old country, signed on with the army as a scout and then ordered west to Fort Assiniboine in Montana Territory, the largest army post in the country at that time. The gigantic fort had been established as a defensive response to Custer's demise at Little Bighorn, anticipating further Indian uprisings that never materialized.

As a boy and later as a young man, Pete often accompanied his father to Cantana on army business, eventually coming to live with Marshal Brenton and his wife when his parents passed away. He had a lot of regard for the old marshal, who had taken him under his wing and treated him as a son. On Pete's twenty-first birthday, the marshal made him his deputy. But Pete knew that the marshal might not be around forever. He frequently spoke of retirement and taking his wife, Melinda, west to Oregon. Pete hoped that he would be asked to take over the job on Marshal Brenton's recommendation, but Brenton was silent on the subject. Pete was sure he was capable, but even though he was an experienced lawman in his own right, he felt the marshal didn't have enough confidence in him. He hoped this trust would come in its own time.

But would there be a town left to marshal in? The number of taxpaying citizens was steadily dwindling, so there mightn't be enough money to pay someone to enforce the law. When and if this happened, Pete had it in his mind to apply to the army for a job as a scout, taking advantage of the name his father had made for himself and his own skill as a lawman and tracker.

It was late afternoon, and Marshal Brenton had not yet returned from the ranch southeast of town in the direction of Twete, a small prairie town almost as isolated as Cantana. He had gone to arrest a man caught stealing a horse and to bring him back for trial. Stealing a man's horse in this part of the country was the same as murdering him or leaving him to perish alone on the prairie without food or water. Justice was usually dispensed rapidly, albeit often crudely—a horse thief might be shot or hanged in some lonely coulee and that would be that, dispatched with no more thought than it took to ring the neck of a chicken for Sunday dinner. This particular rancher, a hard but fair man, respected the law and had chosen to take the thief into custody, sending word by the infrequent stage for the marshal to come and get his prisoner.

He will probably be hanged anyway, Pete Randers thought, *but at least he will get a trial first.* Pete considered the man lucky, for there were several ranches in that part of Choteau County, and he had never known any of them to turn a horse thief or cattle rustler over to the authorities.

Pete tossed several chunks of precious coal into the large potbellied stove of the jailhouse, closing the heavy cast-iron door with a clang. Snow would be falling soon, and the town was expecting a large delivery of coal to get them through the winter before the ground became too soft and muddy for the large, heavy freight wagons. If it did not come, the citizens would be forced to begin stripping the lumber from the deserted buildings for firewood, accelerating the town's inevitable fate. Ironically and in a certain sense, the town of Cantana fed off of itself. A cottage industry had developed of dismantling buildings and selling the bricks and lumber to some of the yet viable towns along the Hi-line. This partially explained how Montana could have so many towns existing as names only on a few old weathered maps.

Pete filled the old coffeepot, burnt black from years of use, from the water bucket on the floor and dumped in fresh grounds from the wooden drawer of the coffee grinder, setting it on the stove to boil. He had just returned from supper with the Granfields, who owned the hotel at the edge of town. Granfield House, as it was called, was a sleepy enigma and a shadow of its former self. Once a boisterous saloon, around-the-clock gambling house, and sometime house of ill repute, it now served as the only public dining establishment and hotel in town, and at other times, as a church, town hall, school, newspaper office, or courtroom.

The Granfields had been one of the last families to settle in the town of Cantana soon after its existence was pronounced terminal. Of particular interest to Pete was the pretty young Alice—adopted daughter of Richard and Miriam Granfield and schoolteacher to the several children living in and around the town. There was no proper schoolhouse, so Alice taught her few students in one of the many downstairs rooms which also served as a meeting place for church on Sundays, when and if a preacher was available.

There was no regular church pastor in Cantana. Instead, a Methodist preacher came through town every month or so on his circuit, which wound back and forth along the Hi-line. He would preach on Sunday and then stay for a day or two, teaching and counseling with those in need, and then move on to the next town on his route. The other Sundays, Alice's adopted father might fill in, preaching the morning sermon and teaching Sunday school.

Alice's birth parents had been killed in western Illinois twenty years before in a tragic accident. She was but a little girl then. The Granfields found her in an orphanage in St. Louis where she had been taken. Formally educated in the East, she had added to her duties and responsibilities that of editor of the *Cantana Prairie Press*, the town's monthly newspaper. She was also the recorder of minutes at the infrequent town meetings. There was admittedly not much business to record, but she felt if she continued to publish the paper and hold town meetings, perhaps the spirit of Cantana would not die after all.

Alice was a little too religious to suit Pete, always needling him about his "eternal destiny" and things like that, but friends, and especially lady friends, were few on the prairie. There was something about Alice. Pete liked her, and she did not discourage him.

Pete was almost twenty-six years old, well over six feet tall, broad shouldered and handsome. He had sandy brown hair and a dark brown handlebar mustache that drooped at the corners of his mouth, giving him the serious, brooding look of a lawman. Pete was generally good-natured and a man of character, but duty came first with him, and Alice or no, it always would.

As Pete waited up for the marshal's return, there came a dull knock at the door, barely audible above the howl of the wind.

"C'mon in," he shouted, leaning forward, letting his chair come to rest on all four legs with a thud. "Door's open!"

The door opened slowly, and there stood a middle-aged man and woman, blinking at the young deputy who sat before them. Their hesitation let in a blast of cold air, blowing a few papers off the desk which stood near the corner beside the stove.

"Close the door, folks! Yer lettin' the heat out, and it's mighty hard to come by," Pete barked with some irritation.

The man grumbled something under his breath as he turned to push the door closed against the pressure of the wind. "We are the Farnsworths, Marshal. We need to speak with you."

"Firstly, Marshal Brenton is out of town, being I'm his deputy. Can I help you with somethin'?" Pete said, standing up and placing several chairs next to the stove. He noticed the lady shivering. "Ma'am, scoot up here close to the heat and have some of this coffee. It ain't much, but it's hot."

The woman smiled. "Thank you, young man. We've come a long way, and it's particularly cold out there."

The Farnsworths were a well-dressed couple, and it was obvious they came from money. Mr. Farnsworth, who looked older than his wife, was slightly corpulent with short, stubby legs. He wore an expensive, gray three-piece suit, a gold watch and chain, and a long, fur-lined coat fastened with large buttons. Sporting a thin mustache and the air of a successful, educated businessman, he removed his derby hat, revealing a few strands of dark brown hair combed across his large, balding head.

Mrs. Farnsworth, in contrast, was tall, thin, and delicate, and though she could obviously afford to wear expensive clothing, she dressed conservatively, wearing only a simple practical black dress and heavy fur coat. Her dark blue hat was unpretentious, with a sensibly wide brim, adequate to cover her head and keep out the weather, secured with a long brass pin decorated with a sky-blue glass bauble. A woolen scarf wrapped tightly over the top of her hat and tied in a bow under her chin. Tresses of gray-streaked hair escaped her hat and fell across her forehead, failing to hide the lines of care on her otherwise attractive face.

The man looked at Pete, clearing his throat loudly—his jaws stiff from the cold. "Deputy, we have just come in on the stage which lost a wheel outside of town. It was most inconvenient, for we had to walk the remainder of the way." He sniffed, his voice and manner equally stuffy, as Pete handed him a steaming cup of coffee. Farnsworth took the cup and handed it to his wife, who quickly held it against her cheek, squeezing her tearing eyes shut to let the warmth soak in.

"Sir, my wife and I have come from Chicago to this wilderness for one reason—to find my brother and his wife and daughter. They came out here several years ago as missionaries to some Nez Perce Indians camped out in the Bear Paw Mountains. Why my brother chose to do such a foolhardy thing as ministering to Indians, I'll never know, but he's still my brother. His custom has been to send me a letter every couple of months to let me know how he fairs. One of their Indians walks it out to the stage or to some isolated post office, I suppose. I hadn't received one in quite some time and so made inquiries through their mission board but they haven't heard anything either. Then several weeks ago I received a mysterious letter from my niece. It must have gotten lost in transit because it is dated from many months ago. I fear that something has gone terribly wrong."

Pete folded his hands in his lap and said nothing for several moments. Most of the Indians he knew about were scattered on reservations. He had heard over the years of a few Indians living independently in the mountains in

Choteau County, but whether they were Blackfeet, Gros Ventre, Cree, Crow, Assiniboine, or even Nez Perce he had no idea—they were all the same to him. Not considered troublesome, they were out of sight and out of mind for the most part, and folks left them alone. When he was a younger man, he would sometimes see an Indian sitting on a pony, silhouetted against the evening sky on the outskirts, or walking into town to trade for tobacco and other supplies. But he hadn't seen any recently and sincerely doubted these particular Indians were Nez Perce. The army had made them all leave the area years ago. He was, however, surprised indeed to hear that white people might be living there with them in the Bear Paws.

"What do you want from me, Mr. Farnsworth?"

"I want you to organize some men to go look for them. I thought that perhaps you and your marshal and a couple of cowboys might go and bring them back home. They have been at this farce long enough, and I don't want my flesh and blood left here any longer in this country that's been forsaken by God and all that is holy. Maybe your town doctor might go too. We have to know what has happened to them, and I believe it's your duty to help us!" Farnsworth struck the edge of Pete's desk with an open hand upon uttering his last word.

Pete was immediately put off by Farnsworth's insistent manner. The man was a peacock, strutting and loud, and Pete purposely let his face show his irritation and lack of empathy. "I don't need you to tell me my duty, Farnsworth. You realize that we are expecting snow any day now, and it is surely snowing already in the mountains? And besides, this town doesn't have a doctor. Closest one is in Havre, or Chinook maybe . . . certainly at Fort Assiniboine. But they're not going to leave their duties and go to the mountains for a couple of white folks unwise enough to live in Indian country. And by the way, we have church here every Sunday, so you see, Mr. Farnsworth—God has not forsaken us!"

"But surely someone must go! I am prepared to pay them well—in gold if it comes to that!" Farnsworth exclaimed with his thin nose in the air, his voice rising again in frustration.

"Mister, what good is gold if you're dead?" Pete said dryly, raising his voice to the level of Farnsworth's. Then, taking a deep breath, he leaned forward, looking directly into the man's eyes. "The truth is, Farnsworth, nobody is gonna risk their lives this time of the year, especially for a few Indians and a couple of missionaries. I won't, the marshal won't, and nobody in this town is going to either. All of the men workin' on ranches outside of town are set for the winter, and none of them will leave a warm bunkhouse with the promise of three hot meals a day to freeze to death lookin' for some Indian Sunday school teachers. You haven't any evidence of foul play, have you?"

Farnsworth reached into the pocket of his suit coat and pulled out an envelope. "Read this, Deputy! This is the letter I received from my niece several weeks ago, and there is a map attached. And those brown smudges along the bottom appear to be dried blood. Do you need me to read it to you?"

"No, thank you, Farnsworth. Some of us out here in this 'God-forsaken country,' as you call it, have learned to read and write," Pete said, snatching the envelope from the man and reading it as if he had vinegar on his tongue:

Dear Uncle Samuel,

Trouble here! Send help at once, or it will be too late. I fear they will be back again, and all will be lost. Follow the map and our braves will meet you.

Please hurry!

Judith

"Who are *they?*" Pete asked, tapping the envelope on the desktop.

"I don't know. Judith is my niece, and although I have never met her, I want her back! There is obviously something amiss. Why didn't my brother write the letter himself, and why is there blood on this envelope? You must know someone who will go! They are certainly in trouble, and I'm desperate to know what has occurred." Farnsworth leaned forward in his chair, his emotional plea hanging in the air like a bad odor.

Pete folded the letter and stuffed it back into its envelope, lifting an eyebrow. "You say you received this several weeks ago. Why all of a sudden is there such urgency? Why didn't you come right away?"

Farnsworth leaned back. "Well, my affairs would not let me come right away . . . but that's not the issue here. I am asking for your help now, Deputy!"

Pete leaned back in his chair again, contemplating the Farnsworths' plight. "There are other towns around the Bear Paws, and along the Hi-line, and they are much closer to where you need to go. How in heaven's name did you wind up in Cantana?"

Farnsworth moaned. "We spoke with several town marshals along the way, and the army too. Like you, none of them were willing to go, but the army did recommend your boss—Marshal Brenton, is it? He apparently has quite the reputation. Won't you speak to him for us?"

"There are Indians all around the Bear Paws, and they would certainly know if any Nez Perce are livin' there amongst them. Why don't you contact the Bureau of Indian Affairs to see what they know? As far as the marshal goes, all I can do for you is to mention it to him when he gets in. I doubt if he will help you. He has his duties and his charge to his own people. I'm sorry, but that's the facts of it." Pete spoke firmly, pressing his lips together tightly and folding his arms across his chest.

Then, with a desperate voice and tired red eyes, Mrs. Farnsworth spoke. "Deputy, you will have to forgive my husband's rather aggressive appeal for help. He is a man of great responsibility back east and is accustomed to getting action and results with his words. If something has happened to our brother and his family, our little niece is still out there all alone amongst those red savages and who knows what else. If she is still alive, she must be brought back for her safety, or she will become just like one of them. I've heard what happens to kidnapped white children."

Pete looked at the couple that sat before him and wondered how they could be the relatives of missionaries who had sacrificed their lives for these Indians. "Sorry, Ma'am, but the rules out here are different. I'm not unsympathetic to your problem, but this is wild frontier, not civilized Chicago."

"Sir, I am unaccustomed . . ." Farnsworth began gruffly, then halted in despair as his wife put her hand on his arm. Slowly he rose to his feet, taking the tin cup from her and handing it to Pete. "We will be staying at the hotel down the street and leaving on the stage as soon as it's repaired— just in case you or your marshal have a change of heart! We will ride on until we can find someone willing to go. Perhaps we can persuade the army up ahead to send someone after all. We bid you good night, sir."

Mrs. Farnsworth smiled and nodded her head. Pete stood up and nodded back but said nothing.

Samuel Farnsworth put his hand on the doorknob and then turned to face Pete. "Here," he said soberly, handing the letter back over. "Will you at least show this letter to your marshal? I will retrieve it just before I leave. Perhaps if he reads it, he may think of some way to help us." And with that, the couple bucked the cold, blowing wind and rain and disappeared into the unfriendly evening.

Tomfool city folks! Pete thought. *Think you can fix anything by jinglin' a few gold coins together. Those missionaries came out here with their eyes wide open—now let them deal with the outcome and not drag other folk into it!*

Pete sat back down next to the hot stove and took a sip of coffee. He had just out argued a man purported to be rich, educated, and skillful in words, but strangely, he felt no pleasure in it. Maybe Farnsworth needed to be taken down a few pegs, but not in front of his wife. Pete wished he had not let his ginger flare up. Regardless of what the Farnsworths were like, they were still folks and were upset at not knowing the fate of their family. Pete tried to remember what Marshal Brenton had told him before in dealing with people: "Words are like bullets, but not everyone needs to be shot!"

* * *

Just before midnight, as the wind blew colder and the rain mixed with sleet and snow, two men on horseback rode down the muddy main street and stopped in front of the jail. Pete had dozed off in his chair, but hearing the snorting of the horses, he quickly stood up and walked to the window. It was Marshal Brenton with his prisoner.

Pete opened the door as the marshal thrust his man into the room—his clothes soaked through to the skin from the heavy late-autumn rain. Unlocking the man's hand irons, Brenton gave the prisoner a heavy wool blanket and led him through an open cell door, clanging it shut. "Now, son," he said to the young man, "strip down your wet clothes and pile them here outside the cell. We'll hang 'em up for you by the fire. Dry yourself off with this towel, and let us see if we can conjure you up some hot food."

"Coffee's hot, Marshal," Pete said. "Did you have any trouble with the man?"

"Not a bit," he answered, hanging his hat and heavy coat and rain slicker up on the wall and tossing the wet hand irons on his desk. "Rub some grease on these, Pete, before they rust themselves shut."

Marshal Brenton looked every bit the typical cowboy lawman. He was well over six foot two and lanky, and his determined, leathery face was shriveled from age and years of exposure to the prairie wind and sun. He was clean-shaven except for a long, gray, dripping mustache with corners that hung to the bottom of his chin. Brenton had retired from the army years ago as a top sergeant, and becoming a marshal seemed a natural step for him. He was a kind and fair man who had somehow escaped the hardness that had settled upon many a prairie marshal, but when crossed, he had no qualms about enforcing the law. Several unmarked plots of ground in the town cemetery could testify to that.

Pete had heard many tales through the years about his boss. One story of note had occurred during Cantana's wild, gambling days, when three men drifted into the sprawling town and took rooms at one of the local saloon-and-emporiums. Marshal Brenton, as cool as a whisper, confronted the men who had seated themselves at a table in the shadows of the dining room, where they were quietly eating their supper and nursing a bottle of spirits. The three men looked up as the marshal approached and pulled out a chair to sit down.

"You boys plan on stayin' long?" he asked, tugging on the long corner of his mustache.

The three men looked at each other with a silly smile. "We're leavin' in the mornin'—headin' south," the short one said, taking a bite out of the thick slab of longhorn that hung over the edges of his plate.

The marshal narrowed his eyes and slowly placed both of his hands on the table to keep them in plain sight. "Then I will take your word for it. Enjoy your supper, gentlemen," he said, standing up to leave. "If you are gone by noon tomorrow, that will be the end of it." He pinched the brim of his hat and left the three men to contemplate what had just happened.

Pete had heard the story told over and over through the years, but when he asked the marshal about it, he just smiled and said nothing. The rumor in town was that the three men were "Kid Curry" Logan, the famous outlaw, and two of his brothers in their early days of crime. The vindictive outlaw, not respectful or afraid of the law in any measure, was rarely known to back down from a fight. Perhaps taken off guard by Brenton's boldness and way and content on finishing his supper, Kid Curry had decided to just let it go. Logan was reputed to have killed several lawmen over the years before ending his own life with a bullet through the head. The young deputy knew he would probably never know the whole truth, but if it had happened, Marshal Brenton would be the one man capable of doing it.

Marshal Brenton stood before the hot stove holding his hands out to thaw, continuing his conversation with his deputy. "Just a young bewildered kid, half-scared to death, and very worried we're gonna hang him. He claims he is innocent—was hungry and lookin' to get out of the weather, that's all."

"He'll be hanged," Pete said with a low voice and a shake of his head. "There's not much sympathy for horse thieves out here."

"That's just it—nobody seen him do it. One of the rancher's hands caught him in the barn, sleepin' in the straw. Being a stranger on foot, they just assumed he was there to take a horse. But ol' man Turner had a soft spot for the boy, I could tell, and I think would have liked to let him go if it hadn't been for his men. He had to keep up appearances of bein' a tough boss. If he hadn't turned the kid over to me, his men would have hanged him for sure anyway. The boy certainly doesn't do things like this for a livin'. I've looked at his hands, and they are as smooth as a baby's bottom."

"So you think the case might have a chance of fallin' apart?" Pete asked, handing the marshal his cup.

"Maybe, but you never can tell. I've seen guys swing for a whole lot less," the marshal said, sliding his chair up closer to the stove. "It all depends on how the jury sees it. Anyways, he's going to have to answer to the circuit judge, and he won't have to wait long. Judge Jorgensen was due on today's stage, and after he holds court tomorrow, we might very well have us a hangin'. It'll sure be fun diggin' a grave in this weather if the ground freezes."

"Who is this fellow?" Pete asked, leaning back in his chair and glancing across the room toward the occupied jail cell.

"He says he was just passin' through on his way out east, but was beaten and robbed by a pair of road agents when the train came through Harlem. They took his luggage and everything he owns, then tied him up and dumped him off on a prairie trail east of here. He was able to get loose and make his way to the nearest ranch, and well . . . here we are," the marshal said, taking another sip of coffee and breaking off a piece of cornbread from the tin pan on the corner of his desk.

"Doesn't look old enough to shave himself, does he?" Pete chuckled.

"He claims his pa is a doctor out west of here in Idaho, and he's been his apprentice since he was old enough to carry his black bag. He says he was on his way to some doctors' college in Michigan, but he has no papers or railroad ticket to prove it."

"That's a shame," Pete said. "If we had a telegraph, we could send his folks a message."

"Well, I'm goin' home," the marshal said, yawning and setting down his cup. "Melinda will have a late supper for sure, and I'll bring you and the boy back a plate later. Why don't you give him a cup of that black muck you call coffee and a slice of cornbread to tide him over? I declare, son, are you sure you're usin' real coffee grounds and not black dirt? You could burn the knot out of a pine board with that stuff."

Pete stood up and smiled at the marshal's long-running misery directed at his coffee-making skills. "I'll put the horses away, Marshal. Don't worry about it."

Marshal Brenton stood up to take his coat and hat off

the peg on the wall. "Hang up the boy's wet clothes by the stove to dry out, Pete. I don't want him gettin' sick. Judge Jorgensen likes his prisoners healthy—whether we hang 'em or not." With that and a quick wave, the marshal opened the door and turned his head to meet the blast of cold wind and sleet.

* * *

Pete lay in his bunk, listening to the cold wind shaking the walls and rafters—the only light coming from the glowing throat of the potbellied stove. His thoughts turned to his earlier conversation about the missionaries up in the mountains. Pete knew that the few Nez Perce that survived the Battle of the Bear Paws in '77 had been sent to Kansas and then to Oklahoma. He also knew that some had stolen away into Canada to join up with Sitting Bull, but he knew of no others, particularly any living locally in the mountains. But anything was possible, and a small group of Indians might have gone there to live in seclusion, hiding from the authorities for years. The southern portion of the large army post, Fort Assiniboine, stretched into the shadows of the Bear Paw Mountains. What better place to hide than right under the army's nose? He felt sorry for the Indians, but his feelings for the missionaries were unsettled. The Indians couldn't help being Indians and living where they must, but the missionaries had made a conscious decision to go there and live with them. That was their lookout, not his.

As the wind howled and shrieked through the scrub in the deep coulee just outside of town, his small corner of the jailhouse grew colder and colder. Finally, Pete slipped out from under his covers to toss more coal onto the dying fire of the stove. Normally, he would have banked the fire and let it be, but he knew the boy sleeping in the cell was chilled to the bone. He walked over and checked on him. He was snoring away in his exhaustion, and Pete quickly returned to his bunk.

So his pa is a doctor, eh? Pete thought, turning his face to the wall. *It sure will be a shame if we have to hang 'im.*

2
Pete Makes a Decision

The dented coffeepot sat steaming upon the hot cast-iron cookstove, its boiling liquid churning strong and thick with fresh grindings from the old mill mounted on the wall. The jail had the large stove for heating, but Pete used the smaller cookstove for preparing his meals in his bachelor life as a deputy marshal. Pete liked it because it heated up fast, had a small oven perfect for baking biscuits or cornbread and an occasional apple pie, and was another source of heat in the drafty jailhouse. And happily, it didn't heat up the room as much during the warm-weather months.

Rushing to finish breakfast before the marshal arrived, Pete clumsily dropped the frying pan on the stove with a crash, burning his hand on its short metal handle. Quickly putting his fingers in his mouth, he mumbled something under his breath as he stirred several thick slices of floured fatback pork in the spattering grease with his knife. Cracking a half-dozen eggs in a wooden bowl and picking out the odd shell fragments, Pete beat them with a fork and poured the mixture into the smoking grease, stirring it up with a dash of salt and a grind of pepper. Dividing the crispy fried pork and scrambled eggs between two tin plates, he set a large golden-brown drop biscuit on each one.

The cloud-covered eastern sky hinted of dawn when the marshal came through the door. The wind had stopped blowing during the night, and a hard freeze had set in. "Coffee's on, Marshal. Open the cell door for me so I can feed our friend here."

The young prisoner, who had said nothing since his lockup the night before, stirred from the warmth of his bunk and blanket as he heard the cell door squeak open. He had a handsome face in spite of his several days' beard and the bruises and scratches from his recent beating. As he stood up and wrapped himself in his blanket, he ran his fingers through his hair several times and took the plate of food from Pete.

"It ain't your ma's cookin', but I think it will pass. Leastwise, you won't get better fare in town except maybe at the hotel," Pete said with a smile. "Anyways, it's hot."

"Thank you, sir," the young man said, nodding to the deputy.

"You betcha," Pete said, "and after breakfast, we have a nice, solid two-holer out back you can use. I think your clothes are dry enough to put on."

28

The old clock on the wall, with its tarnished brass pendulum swaying to and fro, ticked out the seconds steadily as Pete ate his breakfast in silence and the marshal shuffled through some papers at his desk. Pete collected the empty plate from his prisoner, wiped down the warm, greasy frying pan, and hung it from a nail on the wall behind the stove.

Wiping his hands on a small towel, Pete strapped on his gun belt and took his coat off the wooden peg by the door. Quickly spinning the cylinder to check the ammunition, he pressed his .44-40 Colt Peacemaker, once owned by his father, into its holster. Pete liked the .44-40 because the shells were interchangeable with his Winchester saddle rifle, so he didn't have to carry two kinds of bullets. Pressing his hat on his head, he turned to Marshal Brenton and spoke. "Marshal, I'm goin' to take our man out back to do his business and then have a turn about the town. Is there anything I can get for ya?"

David Brenton shook his head without looking up.

Pete quickly accommodated his prisoner, and returning him to his cell, made ready to go out on his rounds. Grabbing the knob on the door, Pete stopped and turned around, suddenly remembering his visitors from the night before. "Oh, just so you know, we had company last night from out east that came in on the stage—a Mr. and Mrs. Farnsworth. They had some queer notion that you would be crazy enough to go look for his brother and sister-in-law in the Bear Paws."

The marshal stopped his work and looked up at Pete, leaning back in his chair.

"You don't say? What would his folks be doin' down there?"

"Seems they are missionaries to some of Chief Joseph's Nez Perce Indians that he says got away after the battle. He hasn't heard from them since spring. I've never known of any white folks, or Nez Perce for that matter, in the mountains—have you?"

Brenton preened his mustache with his forefinger and thumb, thoughtfully mumbling a guttural humph. "Any Nez Perce that got away after the battle hightailed it to Canada to be with Sitting Bull as far as I know," he said. "Never heard of any left behind except those that were killed or surrendered."

"Farnsworth asked me to show you this," Pete said, taking the envelope from his shirt pocket and tossing it on the desk before the marshal.

Brenton picked up the envelope. "Blood!" he said, rubbing his thumb on the brownish stains and quickly reading the letter inside.

"Curious, curious," the marshal said under his breath, narrowing his eyes and staring off in the distance. "It's sure short and sweet!"

Pete took his hand off the knob and leaned against the door. "They are willin' to pay for several cowboys, and a doctor if we can find one, to go after them and bring 'em back—alive if possible, or in pine boxes if it comes to that."

Marshal Brenton quickly folded the letter and stuffed it back into its envelope. "Well!" he said abruptly, standing up and putting on his hat and coat. "Pete, hold off making your rounds while I go run an errand." And with that, he was out the door, leaving his deputy to wonder what was up the marshal's sleeve.

* * *

An hour or so later, the marshal came blowing in through the jailhouse door, followed by a shower of snowflakes that had begun to fall. Behind him was a short, older man wearing a black suit and a string bow tie under his heavy coat. Pete stood up from the desk as the man took off his hat and coat, shaking the snow onto the floor.

"Pete, slide a chair up to the fire for Judge Jorgensen and get him a cup of that stump water you have the nerve to call coffee," Brenton said.

The old man sat down as Pete handed him his cup. "Now Pete, how's about you fetch our young prisoner and show him a seat here in front of the stove."

Pete hesitated as he tried to understand what was happening. "*Now,* son!" the marshal said sternly. "Before springtime gets here!"

Pete lifted the keys off the hook on the wall and slowly

opened the heavy cell door, which gave out a low, onerous creaking sound. "C'mon fella, let's go," he said to his prisoner, the heaviness showing in his voice as he slid a chair near the stove with his foot. "Take a seat here."

"Marshal, what is this?" Pete asked finally, hanging up the ring of keys again.

The marshal's voice was grave. "The judge and I talked it over, and we thought we'd have us a trial."

Pete looked down at the young prisoner, whose face had turned from curiosity to surprise to deep concern. "A trial? I thought court was tomorrow at the hotel! How can we have a trial without a jury or someone to lawyer our man here? We haven't even had a hearing first!"

"Well, sometimes a jury can get in the way of justice, Pete, and he *does* have a lawyer—you!" The marshal turned to address the prisoner. "Son? This here is Judge Jorgensen, duly appointed by the governor of Montana. He is here to try you, boy. Have you anything to say before trial begins?"

The young man sat in his chair, expressionless. He looked pathetic with his bruised face, wondering what was happening to his world. Opening his mouth to speak, he could only manage a weak "No, sir," as his answer.

Judge Jorgensen rose up and sat at the marshal's desk, pulling a gavel out of his coat pocket and setting it and his pipe before him. Then the marshal handed him several sheets of paper and whispered into his ear. Striking the gavel once, Jorgensen began. "Let the court come to order, and let the prisoner stand and state his full name for the record."

The young man stood up on shaky legs and spoke. "Thomas Evans Brumett."

The judge looked the boy up and down. "Mr. Brumett, you are here to answer to a charge of horse theft and trespassing. I have a sworn statement before me from the rancher that says you were caught attempting to steal one of his horses. The circumstances look bad, as it seems you were discovered in the horse barn. How do you plead?"

Brumett gave a beseeching look in Pete's direction. "Now see here, Judge," Pete said. "A man can't be forced to give evidence against himself. Where are the witnesses to this horse stealin'?"

"Quiet!" the judge said loudly, striking his gavel twice. "I'm not asking him to testify against himself. I'm asking him to state his plea."

Brumett wet his lips and then spoke, his breathing rapid and his dry throat crackling. "I am not guilty!"

"Then let the record show that the defendant enters a plea of not guilty. Let us proceed with trial," Judge Jorgensen said, taking his pince-nez from his coat pocket and clasping them upon the bridge of his nose.

"Judge, I need time to prepare a defense. That's just a sheet of paper you hold in your hand there. I want to talk to that rancher and get him here to testify!" Pete said, standing next to the prisoner with his hand on his shoulder.

33

Judge Jorgensen ignored the young deputy. The several moments of silence were maddening! Pete looked at the skinny, helpless boy who stood next to him and then looked or rather glared at the marshal, his old friend and mentor whom he'd thought he knew. The disappointment he felt could not be measured. There would obviously be no defense, even if he did have time to prepare. Pete looked at the floor and slowly took his seat. It seemed that this mock court had been set up to make certain this frightened young man would be swiftly convicted and hanged.

Judge Jorgensen cleared his throat and directed his next question to Thomas Brumett. "Will you waive your right to a jury trial and throw yourself upon the mercy of the court?"

Brumett glanced over at Pete and then threw up his hands. "What difference does it make? Either way I'm to be hanged!"

"Then hearing your plea of *nolo contendere*, I find you guilty as charged, and the court will now pass sentence. Thomas Evans Brumett, having been charged with the capital offense of horse theft and with no defense to this crime nor witnesses to the contrary, I do hereby sentence you by the laws of the state of Montana to be taken henceforth at a time and place appointed to pay for your crime, to wit, by hanging from the neck until you are dead. The charge of trespassing is dropped, of course. Marshal— take charge of your prisoner. Court dismissed!"

Judge Jorgensen, striking his gavel twice, leaned back in his seat, and taking a sip of coffee, he lit his pipe.

The room seemed to spin around for a moment as Brumett felt behind him for his chair, collapsing with a plunk. He had started out several weeks ago from his happy home in Idaho where he had been his father's assistant since he was a young boy, learning the art and science of medicine at his side. His mother had made him his favorite meal, and with teary eyes, kissed him good-bye with hopes that he would return again someday a full-fledged doctor of medicine. Now he was in a strange wilderness in Montana where justice was swift and errors in justice apparently all too frequent. Trying to resign himself to his fate, he rubbed his itching beard, letting his hand slide down to his neck, wondering what it would feel like to hang.

Pete was disgusted, and that disgust turned to anger. He slowly slid his hand across his chest and fingered his marshal's badge—feeling his hand tighten around it with the intention of ripping it from his shirt and casting it upon the marshal's desk. As his fist closed and the muscles of his arm grew taut, Marshal Brenton suddenly drew in a mouthful of air and stood up.

"Now, your honor, I think there might have been some undue hurry in these proceedings. I hate waste, and it seems that hanging this lad would be a waste. I've taken account of him, and I don't think him capable of stealing

35

anything that didn't come from his mother's cookie jar, let alone a horse. May I make a proposal?"

The judge took another drink from his coffee cup, giving the cold, outward impression that he was barely interested. "What is your proposal, Marshal?"

"Well, it seems our young friend here was on his way to school in the East to be a doctor. In fact, his pa is a doctor, and he has been at his side since he was in short britches. Now, that almost makes him a doctor, doesn't it? Wouldn't it be a waste to stretch his neck when there is still some good that might come of his life?"

Judge Jorgensen looked down at his smoldering briar-root pipe, still appearing disinterested. "What are you saying, Marshal?"

"Well, Judge, in the Bear Paws are some missionaries lookin' after some of Joseph's Nez Perce that must have sneaked away during the battle years ago unbeknownst to any of us. We just received word that they might be in trouble. I was thinkin' that maybe we could send our young doctor here to find them and minister to them if needs be. It will give him a chance to grow up a mite and be a man. If he goes and does them a good turn, maybe the court could see it in its mercy to give him a pardon. If we start hangin' all of our young men, especially the doctors out here in Montana, we're going to be in a pretty fix."

The judge was silent for a moment, blowing a wreath of pipe smoke in the air. "Well, son, what do you say? Would you be willing to go help these folks in the Bear Paws? I need to know now—yes or no! If not, then we can proceed with the hanging."

Thomas Brumett sprang to his feet. "I'll go, Judge, but how do I find this place, and how do I get there? I've never done anything like this before. I don't have a horse, and will anyone help me?" His pitiful voice was filled with fear, frustration, and despair.

Marshal Brenton spoke again. "Judge, I will deputize someone to go with him."

After a long silence with everyone staring at Brumett, Pete spoke up. "With all respect, Judge Jorgensen, you're not giving him much of a choice. The rope or dying out on the prairie! He's a tenderfoot and a greenhorn and will not make it a mile out of town before the wolves get him or he freezes to death . . . so I will go."

"So you want to go? I thought you had more horse sense, Pete," said the marshal, sounding surprised. "What will I do without a deputy? Let me find someone to go from one of the ranches."

"Snow's comin', Marshal, and you know as well as I that no one else is goin' to go. It won't be busy from here on out. And if this boy goes alone, you might as well hang him now, because we'll find his bones on the prairie next spring for sure."

"Then it's settled!" Judge Jorgensen said. "You boys take care of the missionaries and the Indians, and I promise to do my part. Mr. Brumett, I will square your pardon with the governor and send it to the marshal, waiting to be claimed upon your return." He stood to leave and knocked out the ashes from his pipe. "I am going back to the hotel for my supper. Marshal Brenton, I'll see you before I leave town."

After the judge had departed, the marshal sat down in his chair and looked at his deputy, who was still trying to sort out what had just happened. "Pete, I didn't mean you. If I can't find someone to go, well, I'll go myself. I've studied the map and know where this place is, deep in the Bear Paws south of Chinook."

"No, Marshal, it's my job. You have the town here to watch and Melinda," Pete remarked, looking at the old lawman at his desk. "Marshal," he said again. "I'm lost for words. I thought you wanted to hang this boy. I'm sorry for doubting you."

"I thought you knew me better, Pete. I don't want to see anybody hang, 'specially this kid here. I got the notion that we could take the rope off his neck and help these people up in the mountains at the same time. Good old Judge Jorgensen agreed with me, and together, we hatched this trial. I know the situation's not perfect, but it gave the judge a way out of a hangin'. Pete, go on over to the hotel and fetch the brother of that missionary. Then we can sit down and talk about this thing."

3
Alice Says Good-bye

The Farnsworths gratefully met with the men later that afternoon at the jailhouse, and two mules were immediately purchased to carry supplies for the journey to the Bear Paw Mountains. It was agreed that Pete and Tom Brumett would start out at first light in the morning, hopefully well ahead of any winter storm.

"I wish I had my leather bag with all the instruments. I kind of feel naked without it," Tom said to Pete while gathering supplies at the general store. "I left it back home because I didn't want to appear pretentious to the others at the medical college."

Pete made a long, sideways look at his newly acquired friend and partner. "Not exactly sure what 'pretentious' means, but just what did you do workin' with your pa? Did you actually do doctorin' stuff with patients or just carry his bag and peek over his shoulder?"

Tom smiled. "I started going on calls with my father when I was about eight years old and did carry his bag

39

quite a bit. Slowly over the years, however, he allowed me to help him, until in time, I went out on calls and made rounds by myself when he wasn't able. I have stitched up cuts and treated scuffs and bruises, set broken bones, amputated fingers and limbs, dug out bullets, mixed up and dispensed medicines and remedies, and held the hands of people while they were dying. Yes, and I have even delivered a few babies. It's ironic, I suppose, but I've performed necropsies on the bodies of dead men who had been hanged to further my knowledge of anatomy. My father told me that in his opinion, I was more of a doctor than a lot of men he'd seen in practice over the years, but I don't have the diploma to hang on my wall to prove it. Pa received his medical degree in Ann Arbor, Michigan, and I wanted to follow in his steps so I could be a proper doctor too."

Pete and Tom walked back to the jail with their supplies. "Sorry, Tom, that all of this stuff has happened to you. I know you'd rather be at that school in the East earning a diploma. I want ya to know that I respect what you're doin', even though you were sort of railroaded into it."

"I am just happy that it all worked out. Your marshal and that judge did me a fair shake, and I want to do my part. I've never been tested like this before—I'm kind of frightened, but exhilarated at the same time."

"Well, glad we didn't have to hang you," he said with a

grin. "But," he added, "by the time this thing is over, you may wish we had."

"Well," Tom said, smiling, "I'm just glad that Jorgensen is a better judge than you are a lawyer. If he was any other kind of man, I'd surely be on my way to the gallows."

Pete and Tom entered the jailhouse and stacked a large pile of supplies and equipment on the floor in the corner. Marshal Brenton sat back in his chair, putting his hands behind his head. "You sure are takin' a lot of grub along, Pete. Are you goin' to set up a trading post in the mountains?" he chuckled.

Pete smiled. "Since I have the extra room with the pack mules, I'll carry as much food as I can since the meat will keep with the cold. It'll be a chore enough findin' wood to burn without worryin' about our daily bread. Anyway, I may need it to barter some with the Indians."

Brenton sat forward with a thoughtful expression. "Pete, I was thinking, why don't you take Tom over to Doc Blake's old place next to the hotel? Maybe he can find some things he can use," he said thoughtfully. "I think I still have the key here somewhere in my desk."

"I forgot all about old Doc Blake," Pete said. "He was our town's doctor for as long as I can remember till he died about a year and a half ago. His office has been locked up ever since."

Pete and Tom walked across the dusty, frozen street that had been a muddy morass just a day ago. The bitter wind

41

blew in their faces as they approached the old doctor's office. Pete unlocked the door, and they quickly went in.

"Let me see if I can light this lantern," he said, striking a match on the wall.

The room was incredibly dusty, and except for the paper starting to peel from the wall in the corner, it was untouched, as if the doctor had only gone out for his supper. There were shelves lined with jars and bottles of different colored glass. A tall, pale green cabinet with glass doors stood in the corner next to an examining table. A desk with a fountain pen and a dried-up inkwell was pushed up against the window. Framed on the wall hung a dusty brown, faded diploma from a prominent medical school back east. This room was all that was left of Doctor Benjamin Blake's legacy as a pioneer doctor. He had slipped away quietly in death, remembered only by those he had helped through the years.

"Well, Tom, can you make use of any of this? I think that's Doc's bag hanging from the hat rack in the corner," Pete said, holding back a sneeze from the stirred up dust.

Tom took the old, black leather bag from a wooden peg and brushed off the dusty cobwebs. He opened the stiff, dry leather that had started to crack and looked inside. Stirring through the contents, he noted that it was well stocked with most of the essential instruments he was familiar with. "Let me look through these bottles and jars along the wall to see what's still good. I may be able to put together some of the things I can use."

"Well then, Doc, I'll go back to the marshal's office. You lock up when you're through," Pete said, tossing the key on the desk.

"I'm not a bona fide doctor yet, deputy. Are you sure it's wise to leave me here alone—out of your sight, that is?"

"I'm not worried about it," Pete answered. "I never really thought you were a horse thief, and if you were, you weren't much of one. I have a mighty encouragin' feelin' about you, Tom. And you can call me Pete, okay?"

Tom smiled and nodded as Pete closed the door behind himself.

* * *

Later that evening as the sun set, Pete and Tom made ready for supper. The wind had subsided enough to let the stove heat the marshal's office to a toasty warm. Pete lifted the heavy lid on his cast-iron Dutch oven to check the meat, and a flash of fragrant steam rose up in his face. He forked the large slab of beef that had been simmering for hours in dark brown gravy with small onions and several cloves of crushed garlic, a sprig of dried sage, and several parsnips from Pete's small garden patch behind the jail.

"As soon as the biscuits are done, we can eat. I hope you like longhorn. It's all we got today. One of the local ranchers still has a small herd of 'em. The meat can be tough if you don't pound it and cook it long enough," Pete said.

"It smells wonderful—just like Ma's kitchen. I sure do miss the folks back home."

Pete beamed at the compliment. "Aw, you'll see 'em one day soon. While you're waitin', you can drag that cot out of the cell and put it by the stove. I have an extra pair of long-handled underwear you can have too. You're a little shorter than I am, but they should fit. The flannel is itchy, but you're gonna need all the help you can keepin' warm on this here trip." As he talked, he took a jar of dewberry jam and a slab of butter covered in a cloth from the shelf.

Pete and Tom sat next to the hot stove eating their supper. Except for breakfast, this was the first full meal Tom had eaten in days. His captors and accusers had tied him to a chair in the bunkhouse, and not willing to waste good food on a condemned man, they fed him only scraps. He was amazed at how quickly his prospects had changed and was determined to make the most of it by earning the trust that had been bestowed upon him.

"Pete, do you think we can find these missionaries in the mountains?" he asked, setting his tin plate on the edge of the marshal's desk.

"I 'spect so. The important question is—what do we do once we find 'em?"

Tom smiled, stretching his arms behind his head. "I think it's strange that Farnsworth stopped getting letters from them all of a sudden and then out of the blue, he gets this one from his niece. What do you think she meant when she said, 'I fear they will be back again'?

"I don't know, but don't worry; let's just concentrate on getting there," Pete said. "Pa taught me that the aim of any journey is to get where yer goin'. Everything you do in between is to that end, so we better get some rest."

"Have you ever been to these Bear Paw Mountains, Pete?" Tom asked.

"I went through them a few times with Pa when I was a pup. There is plenty of good flowin' water, rabbits, grouse, antelope, and mule deer. There is everything that a man might need to survive. We just have to get there, that's all, and I'm certain that at this time of the year, there's already snow on the ground. Let's get to bed; nothing we can do about it now." Pete gathered the plates and utensils, washing them out in a bucket by the stove. He then banked the fire and adjusted the damper. Finally, turning down the wick on the kerosene lantern, he crawled into his bed.

"See you in the mornin', Tom, bright and early. I figure it will take us most part of a week to get where we're goin' if the weather holds. Several days more if it don't. This might just be the longest, coldest trip you've ever taken. I hope these people are worth it."

* * *

Tom seemed to have just closed his weary eyes when he heard the sound of a heavy pan banging on the cookstove. He sat up on one arm, and there was Pete with his hat on, standing in his red flannel union suit, cutting up several boiled potatoes in the remnants of last night's beef dinner. The coffeepot was boiling hard, and steam with sputtering drops of hot liquid spewed out of its spout like a geyser. "You'd better do your business out back—breakfast is almost ready. I hope you like beef hash and sourdough biscuits."

"Just so it's hot," Tom answered, clearing his throat. "By the way, can I ask you a question? Why do you have a two-holer out back? I could never understand the purpose of a privy with two seats."

Pete smiled. "I don't know either, but ain't it fancy?"

"I can't deny it," Tom chuckled. He quickly slipped on his boots and opened the back door leading to the outhouse. The stars were bright and the sky clear, but there was a menacing feel to the air as the bracing cold stirred his hair. It was as if there was something coming from the northwest, like a fierce animal they wouldn't be able to control. Pete was right; there was little time to squander.

Soon the quick breakfast was over, and Tom, dressed as warmly as possible with the few clothes left him after his beating, led the two mules from the lean-to in the back of the jail and tied them to the hitching rail in the front. Pete soon joined him with his horse, Sadie, and a spare horse for

Tom from the livery across the street.

Each of the mules had a wooden cradle strapped to its back to hold its particular burden. Methodically, Pete packed the supplies of medicine, blankets, food, and water to best advantage, and then, with several lengths of stout rope, he began to secure everything snugly in place when he heard Marshal Brenton's footsteps against the planks of the boardwalk that stretched from one end of town to the other. The marshal handed Pete a leather bag and two large buffalo robes.

"Melinda made some bread and meat to get you boys through to supper. Just in case you get into trouble, Pete, these robes might keep you from freezin' to death," the marshal said. "You should have enough grub and water to get you through, although the water might freeze before ya get there. Hunt whenever there is an opportunity, but try not to wander off the trail too far. And don't travel at night less'n ya have to."

"I'll be back as soon as I can, Marshal. Thanks for the advice," Pete said as he tied the robes over the backs of the two mules. "Are you sure you're not vexed with me for goin'?"

David Brenton smiled. "I think this trip will be good for the both of you. It will give you some experience bein' boss for when you take over as marshal, and hopefully will make a man out of our greenhorn friend here."

Pete was surprised and pleased to hear the marshal's

words. Up until that moment, he wasn't sure how Brenton felt about him taking his place someday. "Marshal?" Pete spoke soberly. "If all goes well, I hope to be back in two weeks or so, but the honest truth is that I don't know when we'll be back. I want you to promise me that you won't come lookin' for us, at least until the spring. Tom's goin' because he has to go. I'm goin' because I volunteered to go. It's our lookout. But you need to stay here to see to your duties . . . and Melinda. Promise me?"

Marshal Brenton smiled, nodded, and shook Pete's hand.

"Tom, you about ready back there?" Pete shouted.

"I am. You're going to have to tell me what to do until I get the hang of this. I'm not a cowboy, you know."

Pete held Tom's horse while he mounted it. "You will be when this trip is over. I can almost guarantee that it will winnow the greenhorn outta ya. Now take it easy with this filly until she gets used to you. She's young and inexperienced, and I don't know anything about her. If something happens to our horses, we'll be in a pretty fix to be sure."

"Tom," the marshal said, "I have your address back home in Idaho. I'll sit down and write a long letter to your ma and pa explainin' everything. This way, they won't be pining after you."

"Thank you, sir," he said. "I appreciate it, and you won't be sorry for pleading my cause."

Pete quickly put his foot in the stirrup and swung his leg over the back of his trusted horse. He looked at the marshal for a few seconds but said nothing.

"Son," the marshal said, not smiling this time, "You'd better get goin' before it starts to snow. I can smell it in the air. I want to see you both back here before Christmas."

Pete and Tom waved at the marshal as they turned their horses and led the two pack mules up the street. Several tumbleweeds skipped along the boardwalk, and with nothing to stop them, they scudded and disappeared into a dusty cloud across the prairie east of town. Pete noted the rising rush of the wind.

As they passed the blacksmith's shop attached to the livery stable and corral, Pete approached the south trail out of town. But first, he stopped in front of Granfield House. It was well lit, and standing in the doorway with a woolen shawl wrapped about her shoulders was the lovely Alice. She gave a faint wave, and Pete raised his hand.

"Whoa! Tom, I'll be just a spell," he said, dismounting Sadie and hurrying to the front door. Alice quickly grabbed his sleeve and pulled him inside the anteroom, closing the door with her elbow. Pete looked into her beautiful green eyes that sparkled in the lamplight. He had never known a yellow-haired girl to have such beautiful green eyes.

"Here, Peter, I got up extra early and made these for you and your friend. They're fried cakes dusted with powdered sugar—still warm," she said, handing him a heavy brown paper sack spotted with oil stains.

"Thank you, Alice. You're making it awful hard to leave," Pete said with a grin.

"So, Peter, if I didn't know better, I would think that you purposely took on this job to get out of the service and dinner with me this Sunday," she said, pretending to be cross. "The marshal told us what you were about."

"I would give worlds to be warm and cozy with you this Sunday at the service and balancing a teacup on my knee at your house after dinner," he said, holding her forearms in his strong, rough hands. "If there was any other way, I would consider it, but I'm obliged to go. My friend out there can't make it alone. He needs help, and I don't think anyone else could do it but me. Do you think I'm proud?"

Alice reached up and put the palms of her warm hands against his cold, unshaven cheeks. "I think you are a very good man with a lion's share of character and courage, and no, I don't think it's prideful to say what you believe to be true."

Pete smiled at Alice. "Well, I want to teach him to be a cowboy but not kill 'im doin' it."

Alice hugged his neck. "Peter, I wish you didn't have to go," she said, tying her scarf around his neck with a square knot. "Maybe this will help you to think of me. If it gets desperate, remember that I am here waiting for you—and praying for you. I know you get tired of me talking about the Lord and all, but I wish you knew Him like I know Him. You remember what we've talked about and promise me you will think about it and consider it."

Pete smiled, impressed by this skinny little girl who seemed to care for his soul as much as she cared about his person. She obviously had feelings for him and he for her but Pete was hesitant and careful about reciprocating. He needed more time and didn't want to lead her on.

Deep warmth came into Alice's eyes. "I'm afraid you will go away and something terrible will happen to you, and I'll never see you again—ever! I would love to keep you here with me, all to myself, but that's not possible, is it?" Alice closed her eyes and rested her head against his chest.

"You know, Alice, people tend to throw words around with no more meaning than sayin' good mornin' or good night. They really don't mean it, but I know you do," Pete said.

"What words?" Alice asked, not quite understanding.

"When you say you will be praying for me, I know I can count on it, that's all. And now I must go. There is a snowstorm at our heels, but I promise you I will consider what we've talked about. I couldn't help it." And with that, Pete kissed her and waved, quickly stealing away into the cold wind of the predawn. Soon, Pete and his companion and the two pack mules were outside of town, headed south to the mysterious Bear Paw Mountains and to whatever happened to be in store for them.

Pete glanced back at his partner, whose face was wrapped in a thick wool scarf. Tom was counting on him to get them through, and if he failed, it could cost them their lives. For a brief moment, he wished he was back in town in the warm jailhouse or back with Alice. He pulled her scarf up to his nose. It smelled like her perfume. *Perhaps I am a coward at heart,* he thought to himself. Pa had always told him, "Brave men are just men who wish they were somewhere else."

Pete took heart, and as the last shadow of the town passed out of view, the growing dawn made the vast grassy prairie visible. He could not yet see the Bear Paws, but he knew they were several days' ride southwest of Cantana, somewhere in the bluish-gray haze of the horizon.

4
Wintery Blast!

There were no snow clouds hanging in the northwestern sky, but Pete knew that the likelihood of a wintery blast increased as they neared the elevation of the mountains. It was cold, and the temptation to stop and build a fire and make coffee was great. But Pete wanted to get as far as he could this first day while still stopping with plenty of light to set up an adequate overnight camp. Finding fuel was going to be a continuous chore, especially if the ground was covered with snow. He had tied several small bundles of firewood to the mules for an absolute emergency, but he didn't want to overburden them with more weight than was necessary. He needed to direct his meandering path where the possibilities of finding something to burn were best. This would no doubt add more time to their journey. In the old days, they might have collected "pies" or "chips" from the thousands of buffalo spread out across the prairie, or haply find a place where a cattle drive had bedded down its herd for the night. Dried, compressed cakes of manure made a wonderful fire, but there were no more buffalo herds or cattle drives. In a pinch, dry prairie grass could be twisted into straw "cats," but the process was time-consuming and yielded only a quick, hot fire that could not be sustained for any length of time without constant replenishing. It promised to be a long, cold trip if they were unable to make a regular fire.

Pete understood that to survive you had to keep your spirits up, and good hot food at the end of the day was the best way to do that. But just in case there was no fire, he brought along plenty of dried beef to eat. He had been forced to eat raw pork and bacon before, and it was not a pleasure when you had to take deep breaths to keep from gagging. Pete purposely had not shared his thoughts with Tom. He didn't want to put more worry on him than need be, and besides—it might turn out well after all.

It was late afternoon, and Pete could see a dark purple line along the distant, southern horizon. He knew it was not the Bear Paws, but he liked to think it was. Most likely it was just clouds or haze. He had to be careful and not veer too far to the south-southeast, or he might mistake the smaller cluster of mountains called the Little Rockies for his objective. He would check his compass often.

The terrain from the Canadian border (and above it, for that matter) southward to the railway was mostly flat to rolling prairie, occasionally broken up by coulees—shallow, narrow ravines, some with drainage scars on their mostly gently sloping sides. You never knew what you were going to find hiding in a coulee. Part of the year it might be dry and dusty, and then in the spring it might hold a shallow pond or marsh, attracting mule deer, antelope, jackrabbits, and birds like grouse, prairie chickens, partridge, and pheasants. Coyotes, wolves, and mountain lions knew this and might wait in ambush. But on the open prairie, a coulee might be your only shelter from the wind and cold. Small trees and shrubs, long grass or tumbleweeds blown here could be used as fuel in a pinch for a lifesaving fire.

Just up ahead was a narrow coulee with a fast-flowing stream that snaked across their path. Along its narrow bottom were a few scrubby trees, and its unusually sharp sides against the northwest would shelter them from the wind. If the water was cold and clean, they wouldn't have to touch the precious supplies they carried with them.

"I can't believe we're this lucky," Pete said, stopping alongside Tom's horse. "I've been watching the northwest behind us, expecting a cloud to appear, but all we've had is sunshine. Can you beat that? And this here coulee is a rare find." Pete chuckled. "Alice keeps telling me that there is no such thing as luck—nothing happenstance where God is concerned."

"We've gone a long way today," Tom said, pulling the scarf down around his neck. "How about staying on the trail all night to take advantage of this moderate weather?"

Pete stepped off his horse and stood at the top of the

bank, looking up and down the length of the ravine. "It's tempting, but the horses and mules need to rest. We could step into a prairie dog or rabbit hole or meet up with a pack of wolves. If we have to stop and defend ourselves, I want plenty of light to see what we're up against. If we lose any of the animals, we would be hampered for sure. Let's just take it slow and easy, and we'll get there."

Pete and Tom led the horses and mules down to the stream where they could drink and reach the thick grass that had managed to stay fresh and green under the almost ledge-like shelter of the hill. "Let's unburden these mules a mite. We can load 'em back up in the mornin'," Pete said.

"What is it, Pete?" Tom asked, untying the ropes from the mules. "What's so funny?"

"I was just thinkin' of something Alice told me once. She's always trying to tie God into the things that happen to us in our daily lives, you know. We were at the town picnic last summer and saw a stranger whip his horse until he drew blood. Alice begged me to stop him, and I did. She said to me later that part of being a Christian was being kind to animals. I told her I'd never heard such a thing but figured it was just common sense. Then she gave me a verse from her Bible: 'A righteous man regardeth the life of his beast.'" Pete chuckled and shook his head. "No foolin'— them words are in the Bible! Every time I put Sadie in her stall, rub her down, and feed her, I think of it . . . and Alice too, although she might not regard it as a personal compliment."

Tom looked at his newfound friend and smiled. He was beginning to sense that the green-eyed, yellow-haired schoolteacher Pete talked about so much had a profound influence upon him—even if he didn't want to admit it. "You are a deep well, Mr. Randers, and I have yet to find your depth. And I can't believe that a man who uses the word 'happenstance' doesn't know what 'pretentious' means."

Pete only smiled. "Set those mules with picket lines where they can get at plenty of grass. I have several old army picket pins and ropes strapped behind my saddle. Let me see if I can get a fire started and some coffee boilin'. Then we can finish up the beef stew and bread that Melinda sent along, and more of Alice's good fried cakes."

* * *

"We'd better enjoy the comfort of this campfire while we can, Tom," Pete said, placing several more pieces of wood to best advantage in the blaze. "It may be the last one like it until we get below the rail line. I'll take one more look at the mules and horses. They should be well out of the wind under the brow of that small hill."

Tom watched his partner walk off into the darkness as he spread the bedrolls out on either side of the fire. They would use their fleece-lined saddles as pillows. Tom laid the two buffalo robes on the bedrolls just in case it got too cold in the night. He reached forward and lifted the coffeepot out of the hot ashes and filled two tin cups.

Pete walked out of the shadows, and sitting down next to the fire, he took a sip of the thick, bitter coffee. "Make sure you keep your Winchester close, Tom. I don't think this fire can be seen from a distance because we are so low, but you never can tell. Besides, wolves and mountain lions don't need to hunt by sight."

"You sure take great store by Sadie," Tom commented. "I saw you give her a parsnip from your pocket."

Pete smiled. "I named her after a cat I had when I was a boy. One day, I saw a mother cat abandon her kittens and just wander off. Sadie adopted them, suckled them, and raised them up as her own. That cat had a lot of character. So when I bought my first yearling—I named her Sadie."

Tom smiled and held up the pot. "More coffee?" he asked, as Pete shook his head. "I'll get a fresh pot ready for morning—not enough left to save here. I figure if I fill it with water tonight and it freezes, all we will have to do is put it on the fire."

"Better get some sleep, then," Pete said, pulling his hat down over his face and his blankets up over his head. "It's starting to spit snow, and I don't like the sound of that wind. It roars along the prairie like a beast with nothing to slow it down. I think tomorrow, we will be pining over the memory of this nice sunny day."

* * *

The peculiar, muffled sound of the wind and the chill of the morning caused Pete to open his eyes. The last thing he remembered was bidding Tom good night. Pulling his blankets securely about him, he sensed that he was terribly cold and could feel the weight of something pressing against his body. As he pushed the covers back and adjusted his hat, a shower of snow fell on his face and down his neck. Struggling to sit up, he realized that he was buried in a drift of snow. Glancing over, he could see the outline of Tom's form under another drift, with only the crown of his hat sticking out.

"Tom! Ho, Tom! Get up!" he shouted. There was a stirring under the blanket as Tom sat up and brushed the snow out of his face.

"What in tarnation . . . ?" he exclaimed, standing up and brushing himself off. "Where did all of this stuff come from?"

Pete chuckled, digging himself out of the drift and looking about him. Everything was white as far as he could see, and the sky hanging gray, with the wind whipping little whirlwinds of snow unimpeded across the prairie. The eastern sky, however, began to glow brightly in a long, narrow, orange and yellow band along the horizon, as if a schoolboy had crushed and smeared a firefly against a gray wooden board. It was snowy and bitter cold now, but there might be sunshine today.

"Well, the joke's on us! We stayed off the prairie to avoid the wind, and now all of the snow has blown into this low place," Pete said, straining his eyes to gaze across the wide open plain. Then his eyes grew large. "Tom, where are the horses and mules?"

Pete and Tom scrambled to the place where they had set the picket lines the night before. They waded though the waist-deep snow to the overhang where the snow had drifted more than six feet deep.

"Sadie girl!" Pete shouted.

With plumes of steamy breath and a few grunts, the horses and mules lifted their heads out of the snow, shaking them from side to side. Pete and Tom quickly scraped the snow off their backs and examined them closely.

"It looks like they are in good shape, Tom," Pete said. "The snow has cut the wind and insulated them from the cold." Pete and Tom took them by their bridles and led them out to where the snow wasn't so deep, and finding the feedbags, they scooped out enough oats from the sack to let the animals feed at their leisure.

"Tom, I'm going to try to get a fire started out of this mess. If you could start diggin' out the packs we took off the mules last night, I'll see if I can get coffee goin'. Then we can contrive something for breakfast. You can't keep warm very well if your stomach's empty," Pete said as he knelt down to dig out the remnants of last night's campfire.

As the heavy clouds began to dissolve and scud away, the sun finally broke the eastern sky. Tom had repacked the mules and the horses, and they didn't seem any worse for wear. *Maybe they don't feel the cold like we do,* he thought. Tom walked up to the fire and sat on the edge of his saddle. Pete had been able to rekindle the fire and stoke it into a cheery blaze, and the sight of the boiling coffeepot made him smile. Pete had taken the flat lid from his Dutch oven, and setting it directly on the fire, was using it as a griddle to fry pancakes and several slices of thick bacon.

"Pancakes?" Tom exclaimed. "These taste like sourdough. How are you able to make sourdough out here in the cold?"

Pete smiled, handing Tom a heaping plate. "I hope you like butter and sorghum molasses. That's the way I always eat 'em. Sourdough is easy to make if you know how to keep the starter jar warm."

Tom's puzzled look showed he didn't understand. Pete stood up and unbuttoned his coat and shirt. There, against the warmth of his chest and hanging from his neck by a length of stout cord, was a quart-sized glass jar with a lid held on by a heavy wire clamp. Pete opened the lid, and Tom could smell the pungent odor of a working sourdough mother. "When I want to make biscuits or pancakes, I take out a dab and mix it with flour and warm water, and there you have it. I just add some flour and water back in the jar when I'm done, give it a stir and time to work a mite, and

61

it's ready for the next time. This particular batch is from the first one that Ma kept in her kitchen years ago." Pete put the jar back in its warm place and rebuttoned his heavy coat.

Tom tasted the pancakes and bacon. They were delicious and more of a meal than he had hoped for on this particular day. It was then he realized that Pete was more than just some simple cowboy deputy marshal. He was the real article—talented, trustworthy, and resourceful.

After breakfast, Pete and Tom led the mules and horses out of the snowy ravine onto flat, open ground. The gray clouds were gone now, and the sun shone dazzlingly white against the snow-covered prairie. Repacked and ready to go, they set out again to follow the purple line along the southern horizon, beginning the second day's journey of their task.

After several hours of trudging across the barren landscape without the sight of a tree or bush and no signs of life, Pete was surprised that they had not seen any animals, even birds. He had counted on being able to get some fresh meat on the trail to supplement what they had brought along, but there was nothing, not even a stray jackrabbit. The buffalo were all gone from Montana except for a few small herds collected by private ranchers. Pete knew that it would be a miracle if he ever saw one again in the wild. The deer and antelope were no doubt huddled in low places out of the wind, and they would only encounter them if they happened to walk right up on them. They might by chance find some stray cattle belonging to one of the several ranchers in the area, but Pete would only shoot one if they were starving.

He could sure use a hot cup of coffee and the last of Alice's sugary cakes, but they did not dare stop until they could find a suitable place to settle in out of the wind. They had not crossed a single coulee or low spot where they could make camp since early that morning, and the intense sunlight against the snow was like a steady lightning flash. Pete closed his eyes, and when he opened them again, the brightness lasted as a burning red glow under his eyelids. Looking back at Tom, he noticed that he kept rubbing his eyes.

"How we doin', Tom?" he asked, guiding Sadie alongside his companion's horse."Oh, it's this cold air, I suppose. Makes my eyes sore like I have sand in them."

"Let's have a look," Pete said, reaching across and looking into Tom's face. His eyes were red and dripping with moisture. It was as he suspected. Tom's eyes were suffering from the tell tale signs of snow blindness. "I think we'd better stop here for a spell to feed and rest the animals."

Pete dismounted Sadie, and after unrolling the dark blue wool blanket he had fastened behind his saddle, he spread it out on the frozen prairie and cut out two long strips about four inches wide. He then made two slits in each one, about two inches apart.

"Here, Tom, put this on."

"What is it?" Tom asked, examining the piece of cloth.

"Here, do like this," Pete said. He wrapping his around his head and tied it in the back. He then centered the slits over his eyes and adjusted the holes so he could peer through them. "These are masks to help keep the bright light out of your eyes. You will be snow-blind by the end of the day if you don't wear it. It's an old Indian trick I learned from my pa."

Tom followed his partner's example and tied the cloth around his head. "That's a whole lot better. How come you weren't bothered by the sunlight? Am I that much of a tenderfoot?"

Pete shook his head. "It bothers me too, but I've learned to cover my eyes and let the horse do the seeing while I ride. I guess I should have warned you it might happen. I've seen men laid up for days with snow blindness. Now let's contrive some blinders for the horses and mules. I'm not sure how much the brightness affects 'em, but just in case, let's not take any chances."

Pete and Tom tied a length of the cloth around the heads of the mules and horses to block out the reflected sunlight from off the prairie and then continued their journey. *I've got to take care. There's no room for mistakes,* Pete thought, somewhat disappointed in himself for not having anticipating this little crisis.

* * *

As the sun was within an hour of setting, Pete made the decision to stop in the only low spot he could find that afforded some protection from the wind. It was not as deep as the one they had camped in the previous night, but it would have to do. Tom picketed the animals where the prairie grass was thickest and sticking up out of the snow. Pete took a small shovel from one of the mule's packs and dug a fire pit.

The sod was thick but not so hard because it had not yet frozen deeply, and after a half-hour of digging, Pete wiped the sweat from his forehead and said, "That'll have to do. I'll burn what wood we have left with some prairie grass to get us a pot of coffee, but I'm afraid there'll be no big meal tonight. I have some eggs left; maybe I can scramble a few if I can get the pan hot enough. Let's unpack those mules and use the baggage as a windbreak around the fire while it lasts. I'm glad to have those buffalo robes the marshal gave us. But after tonight, there will be no more hot meals until we can locate some fuel."

5

The Luxury of Fear

The next morning was more of the same as the bitter morning light chased the stars from the clear sky overhead. Pete and Tom repacked the mules and gave each of the animals a feed bag full of oats. The men gnawed on a few strips of dried beef and stuffed some extra in their pockets for the trail. Tom had kept the coffeepot next to him during the night to keep it from freezing, so they each had a cup of cold coffee to wash down the leatherlike beef.

"We might as well tie the blinders on the animals again. I declare, I hope we see some trees soon or come upon a deep coulee. This prairie must be what it looks like on the moon without the cheese," Pete said, mounting his horse and wrapping his woolen scarf around his face. It looked like the sun would be as bright today as yesterday.

"Pete, do you think we will be able to find some way to make up a fire soon? There's got to be something up ahead," Tom inquired with a slight apprehension in his voice. Pete didn't believe that Tom was afraid, but like any man lacking the experience and knowledge to survive, he was concerned about what he didn't know.

"Oh, sure! We should be able to mosey out of this before too long. There is bound to be fuel and shelter ahead," Pete answered, trying to sound confident and encouraging. Changing the subject, he asked, "Have you thought about what you're going to do when this is all over?"

"Well, the first thing I will do is get my hands on that pardon. Then I'll try to get word to my folks that I'm all right and earn enough money to get a train ticket to Michigan," Tom answered thoughtfully.

"Farnsworth said there was some money in this, and likely he can afford it. It is rightly yours for lookin' for his brother. He doesn't have to know about your arrest or the deal with the judge," Pete said, glancing back at the two pack mules laboring along behind them.

"We'll know when we are getting nearer our destination, Tom, when we cross the railroad tracks and the Milk River. There should be trees for firewood soon and perhaps some game to shoot. A seven- or eight-pound jackrabbit would make us a good meal. And by then, we should be able to see the mountains southwest of here. It will give us something to look forward to, anyway."

* * *

The long day wore on as they put mile after cold mile behind them—the bitter wind cutting at them like straight razors and broken glass. A high, gray cloud deck had moved in from the northwest almost unnoticed, giving them some relief from the sun. Pete shook his feet in the stirrups and realized that he could barely feel them. The bitter cold made them feel like wood, and he knew he would have to stop soon and build a fire or he and Tom might be in trouble. He searched the horizon for anyplace that would get them out of the wind, but the trail led across a large expanse of featureless prairie and snow.

Pete thought about Alice and wondered if she was praying for them now. She set such great store by prayer that he was almost convinced there was something to it. He hoped there was, because he and Tom were in need of help. Anyway, she believed it was real, so who was he to doubt it?

"How are the feet, Tom?" Pete asked, pulling the frosted scarf away from his mouth.

"What feet?" Tom chuckled. "All I know is there are weights hanging off the ends of my legs. If my feet are still in the stirrups, I really can't tell."

"If we don't find a camp soon, we'll need to dismount and walk to get the blood flowin' again," Pete said, pulling his scarf back up over his mouth and nose. Pa lost a couple of toes one winter to frozen feet and it wasn't a pretty sight.

Several hundred yards or so ahead, with the terrible

wind blowing at their backs, Pete could see a small outcropping of boulders near what looked like an old buffalo wallow. It was covered with deep snowdrifts and didn't appear to offer much shelter. As they approached, Sadie suddenly bucked and reared up on her hind legs. Something had startled her, but Pete couldn't make it out.

"Whoa, Sadie girl!" Pete said, softly patting the side of her head. When he finally calmed her down, he could hear what her sharper ears had heard. A low moaning sound like a rushing of air came from the rocks. Pete dismounted to investigate. When his heavy feet hit the ground, his legs almost buckled under him. His feet stung with pain that shot up his legs, but he felt relief, too—the pain told him his feet were not frozen.

Hanging on tightly to Sadie's bridle, Pete approached the rocks with caution. He followed the strange sound, which led him to a dark hole in the white ground. Picking up a double handful of snow, he tossed it over the hole and was surprised when the escaping air caught it and blew it skyward like feathers from a down pillow. Dropping to his knees, Pete dug and scraped the hole larger with his hands until it was obvious that there was a large, narrow opening there. It was a cave!

"Tom, come here and give a hand. I think we may have found something."

Tom dismounted his horse and stumbled like a drunken man, trying to get his feet to work. He made his way back to one of the mules and found the short-handled shovel. Kneeling beside Pete, he dug and dug until the mouth of the cave was cleared. It was just large enough for the horses and the two pack mules to squeeze through. Pete walked back to Sadie and rummaged around in his war bags. "Ah, found it," he said, holding up a long tallow candle. "Well, Tom, I'm going in for a closer look. I hope I don't find a mountain lion or a hibernating bear. Odds are we aren't the only ones needing shelter."

Pete cautiously made his way through the entrance of the wide fissure, which at first angled downward so steeply that he embraced the rock wall to keep from slipping. Then, sufficiently sheltered from the bitter wind, he struck a match on the cave wall and lit the candle. The place where he stood was so dismal that the light could only penetrate a yard or so. As he began to explore and his eyes adjusted to the low light, he found that the narrow passage suddenly opened up into a fairly large chamber with a high ceiling of about twelve feet. Scattered across the sandy cave floor were animal bones and tufts of fur. Perhaps something was living here in the frigid gloom.

Pete mustered up all of his fortitude. He didn't have the luxury to fear what might or might not be in the darkness. He had to have a fire soon so he and Tom could thaw out and make water for the horses and mules. And a good hot meal and coffee and a night's rest would make their spirits more equal to the task at hand.

71

Pete searched the cave for something that might burn but could only find a few dead roots that had poked down through the thick prairie sod and stony cave ceiling. These could possibly be used as kindling, but that was all. What was he going to do? He would not let the animals suffer— he would shoot them if he had to. But he was getting ahead of himself.

Pete sat down on a flat rock, contemplating their plight, when he noticed some faint markings and dark streaks on the cave wall. He stood up and held the candle closer. A thick layer of black rock snaked through the soft sandstone wall of the cave. He took out his pocketknife and dug out a piece. It appeared to be a thin vein of coal that could be easily extracted with a pickaxe or chisel and hammer. But Pete had none of those things. *What a joke on me!* he thought. *Just the very thing I need, and I have no way of gettin' at it.*

His feet throbbed and ached, and he shivered dreadfully. If he could only get a few chunks of that precious black gold out of the wall, he could make a good, hot fire that would last a long time, but how could he do it?

Pete made his way back up the incline to where Tom was standing with the animals. "Tom, I want you to hold these horses and mules good and tight so they don't get away from you," he said, pulling his Winchester from its saddle boot.

"What's wrong, Pete?" Tom asked. "Is it a bear?"

"No, I think I found us something to burn, but I have to go get it. Stay here with the animals and hold on—they're goin' to spook a mite." Pete felt his way again along the passage until he was in front of the cave wall.

I'm goin' to die anyway, he thought, *so I might as well go down swingin'!*

Wrapping his woolen scarf about his head to protect his eyes and face, Pete cocked the hammer on his rifle. Aiming carefully, he fired a shot at the cave wall. The muzzle blast and flash were terrific, sending chips of stone and particles of stinging dust everywhere. Several more times he fired and then, standing in the silence, he allowed the dust to settle.

Pete retrieved the candle from his coat pocket and snapped it in half to make two lights. Inspecting the cave wall, he felt along the vein of coal, which appeared to be sufficiently fractured. Taking his large hunting knife from his belt, he dug out the powdery black chunks of the precious fuel until he had a fairly large pile on the cave floor. Quickly making his way back up to the surface, Pete motioned for Tom to lead the animals down into the cave. Smiling at his partner, he said, "I think we just might be all right."

Within an hour or so, Pete had a hot fire blazing in the cave that cheered them both. Once the coals settled down, the very little smoke that came from them naturally rose up and followed the narrow entrance to the outside. The smell of crispy bacon, sliced potatoes frying, and beans bubbling in their thick gravy of molasses and onions rejuvenated them both and gave them the strength to go on. *This isn't such a dreary place after all,* Pete thought.

Pete and Tom shivered in their bedrolls as they watched the steam rise from their thawing feet against the glow of the good, hot coal fire. Their feet ached and throbbed, but with stomachs full of hot food and warm blood again flowing through their veins, the two men soon faded off into a deep sleep.

6
Civilization
in Bits and Pieces

"If I had a wagon, I'd take a load of this coal with us," Pete said thoughtfully, holding a lump of it in his hand. "Nothin' beats this stuff for steady heat."

Tom smiled. "I know what you mean. I'm not looking forward to braving that bitter wind again, but at least we have hot food in our bellies. How you manage to make biscuits out here like this . . ." he said, taking another bite of the golden brown crust on his plate, drenched in butter and sorghum molasses. "Yesterday we were gnawing on beef as tough as shoe leather, and I declare, if these biscuits weren't weighted down with butter and syrup, they'd float right off my plate."

Pete obviously enjoyed the compliment. "Well, Mamma didn't raise no helpless boys. There ain't much I can't do, I suppose, if I have a mind to do it. You know, I'm actually goin' to miss this place. It reminds me of livin' in a soddy."

Tom scrunched his eyes, taking another bite of biscuit. "What's a soddy?"

"C'mon, Tom, haven't you in all yer born days seen a sod house? The sod on this prairie is thick and deep because of the prairie grass roots. If you cut it into slabs, you can build a house with it, stacking it like bricks and blocks. It's a little rough and sometimes spiders and snakes like to live in 'em too, but very warm in the winter and cool in the summer. I lived in one for a time when I was a pup. Truth is, if we had to be stranded out here for a long time, I would start building one right away. It would be hard work but would save our lives, and we could get by with it."

Emptying the coffeepot into the fire, Pete stood up and stretched. "You know, Tom, most everything a man needs comes from the ground. Coal for heat and cookin', water for drinkin' and growin' crops, kerosene comes from oil—that's in the ground; and you can make cloth out of flax and cotton and rope out of hemp. Vegetables are grown in the soil, and as I just said, we could build a house out of sod. Remember this: when you get into trouble on the trail, don't look up—look down! What you need might be right under your feet." Pete smiled. "And when it's all said and done, we wind up under the ground feedin' the flowers."

Kicking some sand in the smoldering fire and picking up his rifle, Pete spoke. "Well, we can't sit here in the lap of luxury all day. Best be gettin' on to the mountains."

Soon, Pete and Tom were again on their way across the

prairie. The wind was bitter and cold like a fierce hawk scratching and clawing at their faces, but Pete thought they might be crossing the railroad tracks before nightfall. He could already see a few dark hills along the horizon in the distance but couldn't be sure they were mountains.

"I keep looking for tall mountains to spring up in front of me, but all I see are what look like round hills," Tom said.

"Well, if you're lookin' for what you'd see in the Rockies, forget it. The Bear Paws, especially on the eastern end where we are headed, are just that—big, round hills surrounded by prairie. They do get bigger and higher, though, as you go west."

"I still don't know how we are going to locate the Farnsworths' kin," Tom commented. "The niece wrote that some Indian braves would meet us, but that seems a long shot."

"I have the map drawn out by Farnsworth's niece, and as crude as it is, she must be a young girl, but when we get to the railroad tracks, I will use my compass to set out the direction. I have an old army map with me too, but remember, the next leg of our journey is not findin' our destination—it's findin' a place to shelter for the night. You don't eat an ear of corn all at once; you take it just one bite at a time. On this trip, tomorrow doesn't exist—only today is important."

"You are quite the philosopher, Pete. You have a quote

or saying for everything," Tom chuckled.

"That's from growin' up listening to Pa and Marshal Brenton. It helps to set me straight and keep me on the right path. It's good sometimes to have wisdom ready at your elbow."

* * *

Later that afternoon, Pete and Tom stood on a snow-covered hill several hundred feet north of the railroad tracks. Holding his father's army compass steadily in front of his face, Pete glanced back and forth to some unknown point on the misty horizon. Satisfied, he closed the cover on the compass and pointed off into the distance.

"There! It will be a while before we get to where we want to go, and we'll have to keep checking, but we are headed in the right direction. Just in case you're interested, Tom, we should be east of the town of Chinook right now. I want to work my way south of town and pick up Snake Creek, on the other side of the battlefield where Joseph fought with the cavalry. Once we find it, we'll better know our destination."

"Perhaps we should stop in town and ask around for help. Maybe they have heard something," Tom said, remounting his horse.

"No, we need to stay away from civilization and people if possible and keep our movements quiet. I don't want to meet some folks that might be curious and take our intentions wrong, and I'm not sure what the army would do if they knew where we're goin'. Some shave-tail lieutenant might take the chance to grab himself some glory and go after the Nez Perce. What a feather in his cap that would be! No, we need to handle this as softly as possible." Pete looked sympathetically at his tenderfoot partner. "But I know—a good hot meal in front of a fireplace and a bed with clean sheets would be nice, wouldn't it?"

Pete and Tom continued south of the railroad tracks east of Chinook until they could find a suitable place to cross the Milk River, which meandered back and forth along the tracks nestled in groves of willows and cottonwoods.

"Why do they call this the Milk River, Pete?" Tom asked, observing that it looked like the cambric tea from his childhood days.

"Well, I know that it flows out of Canada, and some say it has clay mixed in the water, givin' it that coffee and cream look. It's only deep in spots, so we should be able to ford it with little trouble," Pete explained, finally choosing a place to cross well south of town. Leading the way, Pete started Sadie into the murky, cold water, leading the mules, who for the first time showed some resistance. "Come on, fellas! It'll be all right!" he said softly to the skittish mules. One of them locked his legs and pulled back on the rope. But at last, everyone was across and no worse for the experience.

"What's that up ahead?" Pete asked, pointing ahead to a thicket.

The men approached cautiously, and Pete stepped off his horse, carefully sliding his rifle from his saddle. Motioning with his fingers against his lips for Tom to be quiet and take care, Pete walked ahead, careful not to snap a twig or branch, and soon disappeared from view. Tom sat still on his horse, holding his rifle, waiting for Pete's signal.

Suddenly, Pete came hurrying back out with a smile on his face. "You'll never guess what's in this snarl of trees! I found us an abandoned trapper's cabin. It's not very big, but it has a small stove and a table and chairs—all the comforts of home, keepin' in mind that I live in a jailhouse."

Tom quickly slid off his horse and led the animals ahead. Pete kept talking. "There's even a lean-to for several horses out back, Tom. We could live here if we didn't have a job to do. Let me get a fire goin', and then we can unpack the mules for the night. Take the animals down to the river for a drink. Spendin' the night under cover will be a treat for them too."

As the evening twilight fell on the small cabin, the men sat at the dusty table, perhaps unused for years. "Bacon and beans and biscuits are all we have, Tom, but the coffee is good, and I declare, I'll never bellyache about my surroundin's again. It's a pure blessing to be in a warm house—weathered old shack though it is."

Tom pointed up to the corner of the low ceiling at a

large, abandoned hornet's nest. Dozens of the dead insects lay on the floor beneath it. "I'm glad it's wintertime, Pete. I'm not in the mood to contend with that."

Pete smiled. "If they were bees, we would at least have some honey to show for our stings."

Tom fixed his eyes on the fire. "I wish we could take this cabin with us when we go. I kind of like it. Maybe someday when this is all over, I'll come back here and go fishing." He sipped his hot coffee thoughtfully.

"Then I'll come with you. Maybe we'll both be married and have a couple of kids by then," Pete said, "and we'll teach our sons how to be men." Pete was smiling when he said it, but the smile quickly faded away. When this was over, Tom would be leaving to go out East. He had grown fond of the young "doctor" in the short few days they had know each other, like the kid brother he'd never had.

"Pete, it looks like we will be in the heart of these mountains in a day or so. I know that bears hibernate, but what about wolves? Have you heard anything about them in this part of Montana?" Tom asked.

Pete set his cup down and gazed at the hot fire in the small cast-iron stove. The wind howled outside sort of wolflike, and with every puff against the mouth of the rusted stovepipe that protruded through the side of the wall, the fire crackled and flared with orange and yellow flame.

"I can remember since I was a young boy hearin' stories

of a race of white wolves that were said to prey upon livestock, particularly cattle and sheep, and sometimes people. Those that have seen them say they roam the prairies and hills in large packs, like huge ghostly dogs with frosted white fur, seeking out their victims as they find them. An old soldier, a friend of my father, said it was nothing to see a hundred sheep torn from nose to tail, not because the wolves were hungry, but just for the joy of killin'. One old rancher told me that his neighbor lost over fifty head of cattle in one night, their throats torn out just so the wolves could eat their tongues. Another story is told years ago that some braves who lived south of Havre left their families behind for several days while they went huntin' for winter's meat. When they returned a week or so later, they found their women and children . . ." Pete paused and looked at Tom, whose face had gone pale.

"Anyway, that was a long time ago. I haven't heard of the white wolves for several years. Maybe they're all dead or left the country, or maybe it's an old wives' tale." Pete folded his arms and put his head back. "Tom, I am sometimes torn between the wisdom of tellin' you things, to teach you and make you ready, or just keepin' quiet so I don't make you fearful and uneasy."

Tom pinched his jaw between his thumb and forefinger. "Pete, I'd rather you be honest with me. Those are pretty frightful tales you tell, but I'm not a kid anymore. If there is a danger or threat, I need to know. I need to prepare my heart. Keeping things from me will not help me or you."

Pete looked at his "kid brother" and smiled. "All right then, Tom, I will be level with you from now on. And if you feel you want to talk to me about somethin'—white wolves and all—I'm here. Now morning comes early, and I'd like to be south of the battlefield by tomorrow night or the day after if the snow's too deep. I'll check on the horses if you want to make sure we have enough firewood to get us through until the morning."

* * *

The dawn was bitter cold and low-hanging gray, with sharp gusts of wind that stabbed like a knife and drained the heat from a man's body in an instant. But inside the cabin were sourdough biscuits covered with a tasty sop of poor man's gravy made from a roux of flour, bacon drippings, and water, and hot black coffee to wash it all down. With the mules packed and ready to go, Pete and Tom reluctantly mounted their horses and left the tidy little gray cabin that had given them a small break from their miserable journey.

As they made their way southwest again, they could see the chimney smoke from the buildings in Chinook in the far distance. It would have been nice to go there for food and rest, but showing themselves and the interest they would engender would only add to their troubles in the long run. The Bear Paw Mountains, which were invisible in the mist and haze, would soon appear as distant hills along the horizon. The men's next destination was the old battlefield less than fifteen miles south of here.

It was late afternoon, and the sun had broken through the clouds. Pete was looking for a spot to rest the animals from their ploddings in the deep snow when they came to the top of a small rise facing south. Pete surveyed the horizon when he noticed a familiar low area with prairie grass so high that it poked up through the snow. Someone had pounded a wooden cross in the middle of it.

"There, Tom," Pete pointed. "That's the place. Even with the snow, I remember it from when Pa brought me here. It's the battlefield where Chief Joseph and the Nez Perce fought the soldiers. Just beyond it to the west is Snake Creek, which will point us where we need to go. Let's go around the field. Many brave folk suffered and died and are buried here, and it wouldn't be right to ride our horses and trample through the midst of it."

Finding Snake Creek, the men let the animals drink and rest. Pete and Tom quietly dismounted and took a look around them, trying to imagine what it was like. Then examining the horses and mules, they proceeded onward along the creek as it wandered to the southwest, hoping to find a suitable site to make camp. The snow would get deeper in some spots as they went along, but the wind would hopefully be less brutal, and firewood and perhaps some game more plentiful.

"Tom, we need to be watchful and make a wide swing up ahead. I recollect there's a little town called Lloyd that we need to stay clear of. They have a post office, and I hear tell of a blacksmith shop, and that means people. Don't be surprised if we find signs that men have been huntin', trappin', and prospectin' as we go along, plus some small cattle spreads here and there. This is not the same unsettled wilderness that Chief Joseph and the army knew in '77. Civilization in bits and pieces is everywhere and people are mighty jealous of their space. Let's make caution the watchword and avoid it if we can."

7

The Tall Stranger

It was late afternoon of the next day, and as the low winter sun arced slowly along the mountaintops to the southwest, long shadows began to creep along the foothills. Groves of trees that had been merely dark places in the distance were now here and there and open before them. Pete led on until he found a sheltered spot along a vertical rock wall with a nearby rushing stream. The rocks were gray and sometimes stained a rusty color, and instead of solid boulders, they were made of many thin layers like sheets of slate, fractured, broken, and falling in pieces to the ground. It was a secluded place, out of the wind, and should make them less vulnerable to any threat.

"Well, let's picket the horses and mules. There's some nice grass in that sheltered, low spot there by the stream," Pete said, pointing to the place. "Then I'll collect enough wood to get a fire goin' and get us a supper."

Tom set about picketing the animals and getting them ready for the night. Pete took his ten-gauge Greener double-barreled shotgun from the scabbard attached to Sadie's saddle and slung it over his shoulder. He might see a rabbit or turkey and wanted to be ready. Plenty of dry wood was available that didn't require the use of an axe, and soon he had collected such a large armful that he was barely able to see over it. As he walked back through a hardwood thicket to the camp, he noticed in the distance what appeared to be a flock of birds scratching around the base of a wild crab apple tree which stuck out conspicuously among a grove of pines. Seeking shelter for the night under the greenery, the birds were perhaps searching under the snow for crab apples that had dropped to the ground. Pete thought he might gather a few of the small frozen apples to make something sweet to go with the stew he was making tonight. As he neared the spot and gained a better view, he suddenly stopped. The flock which he had perceived to be some type of plump songbird were actually game birds—perhaps mountain grouse or partridge.

Slowly backing out of sight, Pete set the armful of wood on the ground. Carefully unslinging his shotgun, he rummaged around in his coat pockets for some shells. "Drat!" he exclaimed under his breath, suddenly realizing that all of the shells in his pocket were loaded with buckshot. They would be fine for deer or other large game, but if he shot a grouse, which was smaller than a chicken, the large buckshot pellets would cause it to disintegrate into a mangled cloud of bloody feathers and dust. In his haste to leave Cantana, he had grabbed the wrong box of shells.

Pete scratched his chin for a moment and then swiftly backtracked to camp where Tom was picketing the mules. Saying nothing, he dug around in one of the large canvas bags until he located a leather bag tied with a strap of rawhide. Finding a sheltered place out of the wind, he scraped out a spot in the snow with his boots and spread his wool scarf out on the ground. Taking out his pocketknife, he dug open the ends of four brass shot shells, pouring out the lead buckshot pellets and carefully refilling the shells from the contents of the leather bag—rock salt. He tamped the coarse, crushed grains of salt tightly with the handle of his jackknife, and then, taking the stub of a candle out of his pocket, he struck a match. Sheltering the flame from the wind, he carefully dripped hot wax onto the end of the shells to reseal them.

Pete didn't have a clue how effective the shells would be, but it was all he had. The grains of rock salt were very light compared to shot made of lead and would use up their power and velocity soon after leaving the barrel. Pete smiled. He remembered from his youth being peppered with rock salt when he and a friend were caught in a farmer's melon patch. It stung like crazy but did not hurt them. But he wasn't a grouse.

Carefully approaching the apple tree again, he got as close as he dared without startling the hapless birds. Taking careful aim at the center of the flock, he pulled back both of the hammers until they clicked into place and quickly pulled both triggers in succession. Not stopping to look, he popped the gun open to eject the smoking casings, and instantly reloading, fired again.

As the grayish-white smoke dissipated in the wind, Pete rushed to the apple tree, stumbling along through a tangle of roots and vines hidden beneath the snow. Kneeling down, he began to sift through the snow with his fingers. To his surprise, he found two dead grouse. Raking his fingers through the deep snow again and again all around the tree, Pete soon collected a total of four of the fat birds. Quickly stuffing them into his coat, he reslung the shotgun over his shoulder and gathered up the bundle of firewood he had collected. Tom came running to meet him as he walked back toward the camp.

"Pete, you all right?" he shouted, his Winchester cocked and ready.

"Everything is fine, Tom. I just got us our supper for tonight. You can uncock that rifle." Pete dropped the load of wood near the fire pit. *Well, at least I know he's not a coward*, he thought, noting how quickly his greenhorn partner had responded to the sounds of the shotgun blasts.

Building a roaring fire, Pete took out his iron grate with the foldout legs, adjusting and positioning it over the pit. Setting the coffee on to boil, he dressed the birds and rinsed them off with ice-cold water from the stream, careful to save the flavorful hearts, livers, and gizzards. As the fire settled down and hot orange coals began to glow, Pete took his Dutch oven out of the pack, wiped it out with clean snow, and set it on the fire grate. Quickly frying up several thick slices of bacon to render the fat and tossing in the giblets, Pete carefully coated each bird in a thick dusting of flour and browned them on all sides. He then poured in several cups of cold water, with salt and pepper and a sprig of dried sage from his summer garden. Clanging the cast iron lid in its place, Pete adjusted the grate over the coals so the delicate birds would simmer slowly.

"That's quite a contraption you have there, Pete," Tom remarked, pouring his coffee and leaning back against his saddle and bedroll. "Did you make it?"

"I had our blacksmith Bill Hester make it for me. The old guy can do anything. I just told him I needed to have a way to cook over a campfire without having to pound metal rods into the hard ground and setting up a bunch of stuff. He came up with this. When I'm done with it, the legs fold up and I put it back in my pack. I'd be lost without it."

"He sounds like quite a talented man. And it's nice to be in a place where we have enough firewood," Tom said, setting down his cup. "I have a confession to make." He reached into the large pockets of his heavy coat and pulled out several large chunks of coal from the cave where they had been several days before.

"It's not that I didn't have confidence in you, Pete, but I

wanted to be prepared."

Pete put down his cup and burst out laughing. He reached into his own coat pockets and produced several shiny black chunks of coal. "I've got confidence too, but just in case, I wanted an edge, so I decided to be ready myself!"

"Let me see if I can collect some dried grass to spread out under our bedrolls to get us up off this wet, snowy ground," Tom said, standing up to stretch and still chuckling over the fine joke.

"That's a good idea, but why don't you dig out those gum rubber blankets rolled up in one of the mule packs? They're worn and cracked a mite but will keep us dry. Most of keepin' warm is keepin' dry," Pete said, brushing the snow off a large flat gray rock he carried over to use as a work table.

After an hour or so, Pete lifted the lid on the Dutch oven to check on the supper. Amidst plumes of savory steam, Pete forked the browned birds, and the tender meat began to fall off the bones. Replacing the heavy lid, Pete quickly mixed several cups of flour with baking soda, salt, and ground pepper in a wooden bowl and added enough canned milk and a splash of vinegar to make a thick, batter-like dough. Lifting the lid again, he carefully spooned it onto the rich, bubbling stew until its surface was completely covered and then replaced the lid.

Taking a small metal scoop he had made for the purpose, Pete heaped a great pile of hot coals onto the flat lid of the Dutch oven.

Meanwhile, Tom scraped the snow around the fire down to the ground and spread out the gum blankets to keep out the wet. He spread out the bedrolls and positioned each saddle upside down, exposing the soft, warm fleece lining to use as a pillow. And finally, he laid out the heavy buffalo robes that would keep them comfortable through the frigid winter night.

With all of the chores handled and the wind subsiding to a light breeze, Sadie with Tom's mare and the mules fed, watered, and content for the night, Tom and Pete settled down before the glowing fire to hot coffee and a good supper. Tom leaned back against his saddle again, holding his tin plate in his hands as Pete brushed the coals from the lid of the cast-iron pot. Lifting the lid and setting it in the clean snow to sizzle and steam, he scooped several tender chunks of browned grouse, intermingled with bits of smoky bacon, giblets, and onion and dripping with thick gravy, onto Tom's plate. Then he dipped a large mound of golden-brown dumpling that had baked and steamed on top of the stew. Tom had to swallow hard several times to keep from choking on his own saliva as his mouth watered at what was set before him.

"You know, Pete, we sometimes have to go without on the trail and chew on beef tougher than belt leather, but when we do eat, we eat like princes!"

Pete grinned as he dished up his plate. "Who'd have

thought we'd be havin' grouse stew for supper out here? Though I've never been to one, I'd say this is better'n some fancy restaurant in Fort Benton or Havre. Just shows you how quickly things can change. Just enjoy it and eat all you want—there's plenty here."

* * *

Pete lifted the grate off the fire and set it aside with the coffeepot and Dutch oven. He would reheat the leftovers for breakfast in the morning. Putting several more logs on the waning fire, he settled down on his bedroll, exhausted and looking forward to a good night's sleep. Tom had turned in and was already snoring; the only other sound was a light whistling breeze blowing through the pines. It had been a good day, and perhaps tomorrow, they would find the path leading to the Nez Perce and the next leg of their adventure.

As Pete drifted away in the frosty twilight, he thought of Alice—how pretty she was and how much he missed her. He held her scarf up to his nose, still around his neck where she had tied it. It was slightly soiled now and had lost most of its sweet fragrance, but she was right—it did remind him of her, and he wondered if she was thinking of him.

* * *

It was past midnight when Pete suddenly lifted his head and leaned on one elbow, awakened out of his weary sleep by something he heard. Or was it a dream? He looked about him, letting his eyes adjust to the little light afforded by the bright stars in the clear, moonless sky. Gazing straight up and slightly southeastward, he noted that Orion had risen, telling him that morning was still hours away. He glanced over at Tom, who was sleeping soundly, huddled closer to the fire which had dwindled down to a bed of glowing coals. The air was sharp and cold, and after several minutes, Pete felt sleep tugging at his eyelids once more. Placing two more logs on the waning fire and stoking the coals with a stick until it flared up again, he lay back down, covering himself up with his buffalo robe.

But there it was again, the sound that had first woken him! Pete could hear twigs snapping and the sounds of rustling in the brush beyond the rock wall. Perhaps it was a family of raccoons in one of their nightly forays. Then he heard it—the unmistakable throaty panting of a large canine.

Wolves! he thought. His skin began to prickle as he slowly rose to his feet, grasping his Winchester by the stock and kicking Tom hard in the side. Tom tumbled out of bed, almost rolling into the fire. Looking up at Pete for an explanation, he felt around for his rifle.

95

"It's wolves, Tom. They must have smelled the food!" Pete spoke in a husky whisper, cocking the hammer on his rifle.

The wolves moved in rapidly, circling the camp in typical lupine fashion, sniffing the air and ground, gathering information and probing for an attack. The rekindled fire had flared up enough to catch the glow in their eyes as they stood at bay, snarling and showing their fierce, dripping teeth.

"Counting their eyes, I figure there are about seven or eight of 'em. No tellin' how many are slinking away back in the dark. They are bold ones too! Look at 'em! No fear of men or fire! Don't shoot until I do, Tom!"

Tom was standing now with his rifle. He shivered with the cold and with fear. He had never seen a wolf before except as a dried pelt nailed to the side of a farmer's barn wall back home. "Maybe they are just curious, Pete. Maybe they will go away," he whispered, his voice quivering like a bowl of apple jelly.

"Not goin' to lie to ya, Tom—these fellows are here to finish us off but good! As soon as we fire our rifles, they will all rush in and pick us off. I don't know how good of a shot you are, but make every bullet count. Aim for their eyes! That's the long and short of it."

Pete stood with his rifle cocked, knowing that any minute the wolves would be on them and overwhelm them. He was an expert shot and would get several of them, but his inexperienced friend and charge was afraid and unproven. They would not be able to get them all, and the wolves that were left would surely make quick work of them and the animals.

Pete was motionless for seconds that seemed to turn into forever as his eyes continually adjusted to the dim light. Then he saw her—an enormous snow-white female standing off to the side. The other wolves gathered about her with high-pitched yips and submissive body language, looking to her for guidance. It was obvious that she was the boss, perhaps one of the white race of renegade wolves he had counted only as legend. But she was no legend as she stood there, staring at him and his partner—cool and confident, ready to lead her minions to the attack.

Pete had spoken with old trappers who told him that it was not unusual for one or two wolves to sacrifice themselves to give the rest of the pack a killing advantage. His eyes were fixed on a younger one that moved in close from the side with its attentions obviously set on him. He knew what he had to do as his finger began to tighten on the trigger—this was it, and he would get as many as he could!

Pete aimed, and as his first shot rang out, the wolf cried out with a doglike yowl and fell dead. Again and again he fired as the wolves began to rush in. Tom fired his rifle into the pack, but his inexperience coupled with fear showed— he hit nothing. One large, dark female came from the side and leaped at Tom, tearing his coat with her sharp teeth, sending him tumbling to the ground. Pete turned to fire at the animal, but he too was overtaken by a brutal hit from the dark. Pete pulled his knife and stabbed and stabbed as the animal tried to get at his throat. He hit the wolf in the lungs, and it gasped for air and went limp. He pushed it aside.

Pete sprang upon the wolf that was on Tom, and putting his arm about her neck, sunk his knife deep into her throat, twisting it and holding on tightly as she jerked and kicked in the throes of death. As he rolled over, he saw the other wolves in the pack moving in. He looked over at Tom, whose face and hands were covered with blood. Pete smiled for an instant and nodded at him in the firelight as if to say good-bye. They were going to die. He wished he could have spared his faithful Sadie.

There was a brief pause in Pete's mind when sound and time stood still. His thoughts raced for refuge to the face of the pretty schoolteacher he had left behind. He desired to smell the fragrance of her perfumed scarf about his neck once more before he perished, but there was no time for that now. Instantly the remaining wolves in the pack were upon them, and Pete felt himself yielding to the overwhelming strength of their vicious attack. The wolf that was upon him bit deeply into his shoulder and shook its head violently from side to side, tearing at his flesh with its carnassial teeth like an old rag.

Pete's senses began to cloud, and he could hear the horrific sounds of terror, almost like a child's scream, of the horses and mules facing their attackers. As the final moments drew near, Pete realized that he must bear the blame for failing to protect his friend. To the folks in Cantana, they would become part of the Farnsworth mystery forever. *At least,* he thought, *I won't have to live with the shame of losing Tom.*

Then there was a loud explosion—a rifle shot from somewhere behind them! Then another and another! The wolves yelped in surprise and confusion, crying out in pain. Pete turned to look around but only saw the remaining wolves fleeing swiftly away, seeking to escape along the gray rock passage. The deadly but magnificent white she-wolf was the last to go, turning for a moment to glance back at Pete. Then, following her comrades, she disappeared into the night and back into Montana legend. Pete looked over at Tom, whose clothes were torn and bloody, but could not tell if he was alive or dead. Turning over on his back with what remaining strength he had, he sensed his mind going dark. With one last effort, he felt around for his rifle but could not find it. Laying his head against his own bloody shoulder, he gazed into the shadows. There, standing high up on a jutting stone outcropping against the firelight and gun smoke was a giant of a man with a black face, wearing a heavy coat made from buffalo hide. The glint of the fire touched the polished brass receiver of his old Winchester rifle, adding to the mystery and horror of the moment. Pete opened his mouth to speak to the dark eyes that stared back at him. "Help my friend," he mumbled, pointing to Tom, and then he faded away into unconsciousness.

8
The Buffalo Soldier

Pete felt someone fumbling with his clothing and slowly opened his eyes to see who it was. Staring down at him and dressing several deep cuts on his shoulder was Tom. Looking around him in the bright light of the fire, Pete was shocked at the devastation in the camp. Bedding was torn, bloody and strewn about like rags and the carcasses of dead wolves lay about them. Pete said nothing as he watched Tom silently going about his work as any experienced doctor would do. Finally, with a smile, Tom spoke. "What do you want first—good news or bad?" Pete could not imagine any news worse than what had already happened to them. He raised his eyebrows and gritted his teeth with the pain.

"I hate it when people say that, Tom—go ahead with it!" Pete said.

"Well, it looks like you will live. Except for your shoulder, which will be sore for a while, you came through it fairly well," Tom said, tying off the last bandage. "My main concern was that no blood vessels were torn. The bites are not as severe as they look, and I have cleaned them well, putting in a few stitches as needed. We need to keep them clean, though, and watch them like any other dog bite. As long as none of the wolves were sick, I have high hopes for your recovery."

"But I thought you were bad hurt, Tom. I saw all of the blood," Pete said, his voice becoming hoarse.

"It looked worse than it was. The blood was mostly from the wolf you killed," Tom answered, covering Pete up with a blanket. "And Pete, I want to thank you for what you did. I froze when that wolf knocked me down. You saved my life for sure."

Pete smiled and then grimaced as a stabbing throb of pain ran through his shoulder. "So what's the bad news?" he asked, groaning at the dull, heavy pain.

"The bad news for both of us is you broke your jar of sourdough," Tom said. "Can't you smell it?"

"All I smell is the blood in my nostrils—like wet, rusty nails," Pete said as he attempted to sit up. "I surely thought we were finished."

"I thought we were too, and we most likely would have been if it hadn't been for our friend over there," Tom answered, pointing into the dark by the horses and mules. Then Pete remembered the tall, dark figure he had seen against the firelight, rapidly firing his rifle at the attacking hoard of wolves.

"Who is he, then?" Pete asked in a rough whisper. "And what's he doin' with our animals?"

Just then, the figure approached from the darkness and looked down at Pete. "Can he be moved, Doctor?" he asked.

"I think so. He's too ornery to be hurt bad."

"Then we'd better leave right away and put a few miles behind us. I have your mules and horses packed up and ready to go. With all of this blood and the smell of death, more wolves may come, or a mountain lion," the stranger said.

As the man disappeared into the darkness again to lead the mules and horses out into the open, Tom helped Pete sit up. "Doctor? He called you doctor?"

"Well, he saw the black bag and how I tended to your shoulder and just assumed . . ." Tom smiled. "A little credibility never hurt anybody."

"Yeah," Pete said. "I *am* glad we didn't hang you."

Soon Pete was on his horse, and Tom, the mules, and the stranger were cutting a trail through the deep snow further up into the mountains. Riding the dark, narrow passages along a noisy stream thick with brush and pine trees seemed an impossibility, but the stranger knew his way and negotiated it with ease. After several weary, cold hours, the eastern sky began to brighten, first glowing red, then orange and yellow. The stars seemed to magically go out, one by one, as if an unseen hand was snuffing out votive candles in a church. As they worked their way through a bottleneck between two rock walls wide enough for only one animal abreast, a fairly large passage suddenly opened into a sheltered valley before them. Surrounded by rock walls all around, the details of its features would remain almost invisible until the fog and mist cleared.

"There!" the stranger said with a loud voice, pointing toward a mound of grass surrounded by a group of rocks nestled in the side of a tall hill. Pete and Tom followed close behind, leading the docile pack mules. Stopping next to the hill, the stranger dismounted and set about tying the animals to several contrived hitching posts. A framework of wooden poles and boards overhead served as roughly built stalls, affording the animals some shelter. To Pete's amazement, fixed in the center of the grassy mound was a wooden door which appeared to be made from the boards of an old wagon. And sticking through the top of the hill was a rusty black stovepipe with a metal cover wired on to keep out the rain.

Saying nothing, the stranger helped Pete off his horse as Tom secured the mules. For the first time, Pete was able to get a good look at his silent companion. He had never seen a black man up close before, only in the distance when he was a young boy living at the army camp. The man was well over six feet tall, very muscular, and he wore the remnants of an old cavalry uniform. His hair was short, and his mustache and beard were closely trimmed, something that a former soldier might tend to do even living alone in the wilderness. Opening the door in the hill, he helped Pete to a sturdy rocking chair made of willow branches next to a small cast-iron stove. Lighting a lantern that hung from the wooden frame that supported the ceiling, the man quickly started a fire in the stove and went outside to help Tom.

* * *

Later that morning, Pete, Tom, and the stranger sat around the stove, each one eating a plate of hot bean soup with chunks of tender antelope meat. A pan of golden-brown cornbread sat before them. As Pete used a piece of the cornbread to sop up the remaining gravy on his plate, he carefully examined the face of the man who had been their benefactor. Looking into his brown eyes, Pete smiled and cleared his throat. "And what do they call you when you're home?" he said, breaking the long silence.

The man did not return the smile but answered after a long pause. "My name is Arliss Moore."

Pete gave a nod of acknowledgment. "I want to thank you for your help. I'm sure we would have been done for if you hadn't come along. My name is Pete Randers, and this is my friend Tom Brumett. I am the deputy marshal of Cantana, way north of here, and Tom here is our doctor. How long have you lived up here?"

Moore took a gulp from his cup and set it down. "I've

lived in the Bear Paws for about two years. Why I am here is a long story. I hunt, fish, trap, and trade for things I need."

"Where are you from originally, Mr. Moore?"

Arliss Moore picked up a long stick with a burnt end that was leaning against the wall. "I'm not wanted for anything, if that's what you're getting at. Don't make me regret that I shot those wolves." He opened the door of the stove and poked at the coals.

Pete grinned as he set down his plate. "What you're doin' up here is your business, Mr. Moore. No insult was intended. I was just tryin' to get to know you better."

Moore narrowed his eyes and spoke. "Then you'd be doing me a favor if you would just call me Arliss. Mr. Moore was my daddy's name. I am from Texas. I joined up with the 10th Cavalry to fight Indians and get away from the way they treat people like me down there. We were called colored troops by the white man and buffalo soldiers by the red man."

"I've heard of that. Why did they call you called buffalo soldiers?" Pete asked.

"We were a curiosity to the Indians. Our skin was dark and our hair wooly like the buffalo's. And some say we fought like the beasts when wounded or cornered."

"That makes sense. My father was a scout at Fort Assiniboine years ago where I grew up. I was just a young man at the time, but I remember seeing lots of colored troops stationed there. Pa scouted for them some; he told me he had a lot of respect for 'em and the way they could fight."

Arliss Moore closed the door on the stove and put the long stick in its place against the wall. "We had sergeants and corporals and privates but were never allowed to have our own officers. Some generals and men in Washington said we were ignorant and lazy—couldn't be trusted to fight when the chips were down, so they always put white officers in charge of us."

Setting his cup on the edge of the stove, Moore looked into Pete's eyes. "I suppose you think there was nothing wrong with that?"

Pete held his shoulder and adjusted himself to be more comfortable with his wounds. "I really don't have an opinion on that because I've never had to think about it. Until today, I have never personally known a black man. But I do know this: a man who has earned his way with bravery and deeds is just as good as anybody else—no matter what color his skin. You helped us tonight when we needed you. You didn't have to do it but you did, and Tom and I are forever beholdin'—buffalo soldier or no."

Arliss Moore smiled for the first time. "And what is a white deputy marshal and doctor doing up here? Are you a posse—maybe hunting a man?"

"We are here to discover the whereabouts of two missionaries and their daughter, supposed to be ministering to a small band of Nez Perce hidin' in the mountains from after the battle. Their folks haven't heard from them for many months. Have you heard of any Indians or white folks campin' out near here?"

Arliss leaned forward in his chair and looked into Pete's face, speaking gravely. "If you are here to round up Indians and take them to a reservation—I can't help you. No one will ever force me to hurt these people again."

"I'm not workin' for the army or lookin' to take anyone to jail," Pete retorted. "I'm only here to inquire on the welfare of the white people, to help them if I can and take them back to their family in town. I have no interest in doing anything more to the Indians than has already been done to them."

Arliss leaned back in his chair. "I know where they are and have traded with them, but that was last spring. I remember seeing the missionaries and their daughter—sort of stuck out, being white and all. She is about sixteen or seventeen."

Pete was surprised. When he'd heard Mrs. Farnsworth talk about her niece, he just assumed she was only a little child. "Were they well?" Pete asked.

"They were well and friendly to me. I counted about thirty or thirty-five Indians—braves, women, and children. The old chiefs are gone now, and the warriors, if warriors they be, are all very young. They've had a bad time of it over the years, hiding from the army and fighting sickness and hunger. And I saw a graveyard there with too many graves in it."

Pete paused, ruminating over what he had just heard. "Do they have a chief? Is anybody in charge?"

"They had just made a young man the new chief when I was there. He is as inexperienced as you could imagine and badly in need of council, but perhaps they saw some potential in him. There are no old ones to teach him and pass on their wisdom and knowledge."

"What's his name?" Pete asked.

"They call him Chief Micajah," Arliss answered. "Some Indian name, I suppose. Don't know what it means. But I've had many talks with him, and he is smart as a whip and full of questions about the outside world. I always sensed he was picking at my brain."

"Micajah is a Hebrew name referring to the Archangel Michael," Tom said, blurting out his words. He had been sitting in silence, listening, and his sudden entrance into the conversation surprised both Pete and Arliss. "I wonder how an Indian living in the mountains got such a name?"

"Well, I heard tell that Chief Joseph and his father were influenced by Christian missionaries," Pete said. "That might explain it. Arliss, can you lead us to the Nez Perce? I promise it's on the up and up."

Arliss stood up. "Rest your shoulder, and I'll check on the animals. I need to think on this thing for a spell. Then I think we all could use a few hours of sleep after last night."

* * *

Later that evening, as the sun neared its setting and the mountain fog formed a hoarfrost on the deep snow, Pete and Tom sat around the hot stove, warm and more comfortable within the sod walls than they had been since the start of their journey on the hard trail. Arliss, their benefactor, proved to be quite the cook as they enjoyed thick mule deer steaks smothered in mushrooms and wild onions.

"Where do you get mushrooms this time of year?" Tom asked.

"I collect them throughout the year and dry them. The wild onions grow along the streams," Arliss answered, taking down a plate off the shelf covered with a white cloth. "Here, try some of this." He scooped out a large spoonful onto each of their plates.

"Pie!" Pete exclaimed.

Arliss smiled. "Well, you'd better taste it first."

Pete plunged his fork deep into the confection. "Apple pie! Are these dried apples?"

"Don't get too excited, boys. They're just wild mountain crab apples. I stew them in honey with a little cinnamon and make a paste crust out of flour and antelope fat. Sometimes a man gets a hankerin' for something sweet, and this fills the bill. Wild blueberries are good too, when I can get them."

Tom chuckled. "Arliss, I had been feeling sorry for myself since starting this trip, but now I feel downright ashamed. This is hospitality!"

"Well, I enjoy fussin' in the kitchen, I must say," Arliss said, settling back with his own plate of pie. "Black folks from where I come from in Texas set great store by their cooking skills. I learned a lot from my aunty Mable who raised me, how to cook and read and write. She told me she wasn't about to have no helpless man hanging about the farm. My uncle Joe taught me about horses and how to hunt and shoot. The rest I learned in the army."

"You sure are an interesting man, Arliss," Pete said, scraping his plate with his fork. "It was certainly Providence that we met you, or should I say—you met us. We have to repay you somehow. But I have a question— how was it you were there when the wolves attacked?"

Arliss smiled as he collected the plates and utensils. "Always with the questions, Deputy. I saw you both from a long way off earlier in the day. I kept out of sight, not knowing your intentions. Then I heard the wolves attacking in the dark. More coffee?" he said as he sat back down in his spot near the stove. "As for paying me back, just treat me like a man, and we are even. Now, we'd better turn in early and start out before sunrise. I have decided to take you boys to the Nez Perce. You will be surprised to know that they are just a few miles ahead of us in the mountains."

Pete nodded and smiled. "I was sure you knew all

along. What made you decide to take us there?"

"I have a good feeling about you fellows. But I do have one proviso," Arliss answered, not smiling this time. "I have taken quite a shine to these Indians, and I want to help them, but if you take the missionaries away, who is going to do that? The responsibility falls to you. You are a marshal, and your father was a scout. Tom here is a doctor. You both have a lot you can teach these Indians. This young chief needs your help. He is afraid and uneasy. I saw it in his eyes. I will lead you there, but you must promise me you will not abandon them. If you feel you owe me something for saving your lives, then this is how you can repay me."

Pete thought for a moment about Cantana and Alice, standing there shivering in the cold doorway of Granfield House. He had planned to be back at his job as deputy marshal within two weeks or less, but he knew now that wasn't going to happen. Circumstances had caused him to become unwittingly involved with helping a small band of Indians who, up until several days ago, he did not know existed. He didn't have to do what Arliss asked—he knew that. He could make contact with the missionaries and bring them back or leave them there if they so desired. He was not obligated beyond that, but now, he must do what was right. He was beholden to a man who had saved his life and was still responsible for Tom, his tenderfoot doctor friend.

"Tom?" Pete asked, turning to face his friend who sat in the shadows. "What do you say? We might not see civilization for a spell, or ever again if it comes to that."

Tom gave his head a shake. "Well, I vote—that is if I have a vote—to go on to the Indians. I have a lot to learn, and maybe in some small way I can help. My folks would want me to. Let's go ahead!"

Pete chuckled. "Tom, up until now I thought you had a head on your shoulders." Turning to face Arliss the buffalo soldier, Pete took a last swig of coffee. "Well, Arliss, I guess you can count us in."

9
Chief Michael's Band

The men had been on the trail for almost an hour when the sun finally burned through the icy fog that hovered above the tops of the mountains and allowed the high blue sky to show forth. The snow was deep but the air not so cold as it had been, since the mountains sheltered them from the wind. The noisy stream that flowed from somewhere further up in the hills seemed to mark their path. "When do we see Indians?" Tom asked.

"Soon," Arliss answered, "but they have probably seen us already."

Privately, Arliss was concerned. He had a good eye for seeing Indians hiding in the rocks but had not seen one yet. Either they were very good at not being detected, or no one was there. If that was true, something was wrong. Indians always posted sentries. Finally, he saw a lone brave standing on a high rock out in the open with no sign of a weapon.

"I didn't expect to see him just standing there," Tom commented.

"I suppose he recognizes me," Arliss offered as explanation. Secretly, he wondered about it himself. *Perhaps there is no one in charge. These fellows are making no pretense of security,* he thought, but entering the camp, the men were confronted by braves with spears at the ready and several more in the rocks with bows and nocked arrows, poised to take the three of them out in an instant. "Apparently, we were allowed to make it to the heart of the camp so they could get the drop on us," Arliss said in a whisper. "Don't move until someone greets us."

Scanning the Indian camp, Pete was surprised at what he saw. He had thought to see rows and rows of white teepees with gray smoke venting from their smoke flaps; he instead counted roughly thirty or forty sod huts with a network of worn paths between them. A few of them vented smoke, but most were abandoned, and some had caved in and fallen into disrepair.

"This is not what I expected, Arliss," Pete said with a low voice. "No teepees?"

"You must remember that these people have been here since the surrender in '77. They were unable to take a lot with them when they escaped, and whatever they used as shelter back then has long worn out and fallen apart. It takes a lot of buffalo skins to make one teepee, and there are no more buffalo. All they could make were sod houses,

116

and they have lived in them for many years. As you can tell, there were a lot more Indians back in those days. Many years ago, so I have been told, the Nez Perce lived in this type of earthen house. So I guess for this tiny band, they have made a full circle back to where they began. If these people can ever find a permanent home and raise some cattle, they will have hides again to make their teepees."

Several braves who appeared to be men of some standing walked out to meet them as a number of faces began to peer out from the door flaps of the soddies that were still occupied.

"I don't see the young chief anywhere," Arliss said as he dismounted his horse. "That's not good." Then, putting a wide smile on his face, Arliss raised his right hand high in the air. "Ho! Greetings, my friends!"

Arliss turned to Pete and Tom. "Stay here until I find out what's going on." They watched their friend follow several braves into a large hut in the middle of the camp, which appeared to be a tribal meeting place. As they disappeared beyond its door flap, all was quiet again except for the curious faces that stared at them from around the camp.

Pete and Tom remained on their horses, waiting for Arliss to return. Pete rubbed his sore shoulder, which was still throbbing with a dull pain. "I'll give you something for that," Tom said, noticing that Pete was uncomfortable, "as soon as we can get settled."

After about a half-hour, the door flap of the hut was thrown aside, and Arliss and the two braves came out and approached Pete and Tom. "Well, Doctor, are you ready to go to work? Here is your opportunity to shine. Chief Micajah has been hurt and is not doing well. These men tell me they were out hunting several days ago when they were ambushed by strangers. The chief was shot in the fray but the rest got away safely," Arliss said. "These men will show us a hut we can use and where to put our horses." Then he paused. "By the way, I sort of put you two out on a limb. I told the Indians that Tom was a great healer and would make the chief as good as new."

Pete and Tom's mouths dropped open. "Arliss, you shouldn't have done that," Pete said with some irritation. "If Tom can't save the chief, we might not get out of here alive!"

Arliss smiled. "Well, then, you're not going to like the rest of what I have to say. I told them that you, Pete, are a great lawman and that shiny badge of yours is a symbol of great authority from the Great Father, the governor of Montana, and that you would track down and arrest those who shot their chief."

"You told them what?" Tom said, staring incredibly into Arliss Moore's grinning face.

"Now if you two will follow me, we can get settled, and Tom can commence doctoring the chief," Arliss said, leading his horse to their temporary new home.

The sod house was larger than Arliss's home back in the hills. There was no stove but a burn pit and an opening in the roof for the smoke to rise. Quickly, they unpacked the mules. What didn't fit inside was put in a storage hut that was connected to the rear of the house. Pete started a fire from the scraps left on the floor and went to find some more firewood when he noticed that someone had laid several armfuls of dry tree branches just outside the hut door. Finding his homemade fire grate, he quickly got the coffeepot going and sought to contrive a meal out of what had been hastily packed away after the wolf attack. As he diligently went to work, the door flap opened, and there stood a tall, young brave holding the hindquarter of a mule deer. Pointing to the venison and then to Pete, he handed it forward without uttering a sound.

Pete smiled and nodded his head. "Thank you!" he said, stretching out his arm to shake the man's hand. The brave summarily ignored it, quickly departing. Apparently, Arliss had *really* put them out on a limb! They were being celebrated as important men with the anticipation of the chief's healing and the bringing of the outlaws who had shot him to justice.

Tom and Arliss approached the chief's soddy, located off by itself behind the council hut. A tall brave wrapped in an old buffalo robe stood guard at the door, holding a long spear. Opening the flap for them, the brave stood aside as they entered. It was dark, very warm, and smoky, and they had to wait for their eyes to adjust. There, sleeping in the corner on his bed, was the young chief. He appeared to be tall and handsome and couldn't be more than in his late twenties. Even on his sick bed, semiconscious and suffering with a fever, he had an air of dignity. A pretty young Indian woman attended him, soothing his fevered face with a cloth dipped in cool water. Startled at seeing Tom and Arliss, she instantly recoiled and hurried from the hut.

"Well, Doc, he's all yours now. Do what you can. I'll go see if Pete needs help," Arliss said, and before Tom could open his mouth to speak, he was alone.

Tom kneeled down beside the chief, and mustering all of his resolve, he threw back the blanket and examined his patient. Deep in the man's left shoulder was an ugly bullet wound—red, swollen, and oozing with pus. *If I could have gotten to this bullet right away, it would have been a lot easier to dig out,* Tom thought, *but now, with all of this festering, he may die!* Feeling the sweat run down his face in the overheated, smoky, malodorous hut, Tom took off his coat and rolled up his sleeves. *This will never do!* he thought, looking about the room. Attracting the attention of the guard at the door and motioning him to the chief's bedside, he tried to communicate. "We must get this fire out of here and get all clean blankets. This place must be aired out and cooled down. I need plenty of water that has been heated to a boil. Do you understand?"

The man only stared, expressionless, at Tom.

"Does anyone speak any English?" he said with frustration in his voice. "English?"

Finally, aggravated and conscious of the ticking clock over the chief's life and his obligation to save him, Tom walked to the hut flap, paused, and then ripped it off its frame. Then he cleared a path on the hut floor and began kicking the burning logs out the entrance, sending them tumbling and sizzling in the snow outside. *Maybe this will let them know I mean business!* Tom thought. Then he knelt down again and removed the soiled blanket, which was covered and soaked with foul discharge from the wound.

Several braves came running to investigate the commotion but stopped short of entering, only standing and bending over to peer through the entrance. "Either help me or get out of my light!" Tom shouted as he turned again to attend the chief. The startled men stepped away from the door. Just then, someone stood in the entrance, blocking the light again. Tom wheeled about, ready to speak his mind, when the person walked into the room and stood before him.

"Who do you think you are, and what are you doing here?" the figure said, speaking perfect English in a feminine voice. Tom let his eyes adjust, and standing there in a ragged coat and dress was a skinny young white girl he judged to be in her late teens.

Tom stood up and looked directly into her eyes. "I am a doctor. Who might you be?"

Brushing the long strands of stringy flaxen hair from her face, she spoke. "My name is Judith. I am a missionary to the Nez Perce. Where did you come from?"

Tom smiled. "My name is Tom. I came here from up north with several friends to help you. Is your name Farnsworth?"

Judith held her head to one side and looked at the young, handsome man who stood before her. "Yes, it is. How did you know?"

"Your aunt and uncle sent us here to fetch you in answer to the plea in your letter. Why did you stop writing?"

Judith paused. "I had almost forgotten about sending the letter; it was so long ago. But it doesn't really matter anymore, because my folks are dead! What are you doing with Chief Micajah?"

"I'm trying to save his life. This place is filthy! I told these fellows to get this fire out of here and let in more light and fresh air. The atmosphere in here is vile!" Tom said, his voice rising.

"Does that require a lot of yelling and flapping about like a goose? You certainly are not a very patient man!" the young woman shouted back.

"I *am* a very patient man when the situation calls for patience, but I need to get through to everyone a sense of urgency, and no one wants to listen. The chief is going to die unless we clean up this mess and tend to his shoulder.

Germs thrive in this kind of atmosphere! And I don't want an open fire while I'm splashing chemicals around to clean the wound. I need fresh blankets and plenty of hot, boiling water. If I don't get that bullet out of his shoulder and clean up the festering, he will die. Are you going to help me or just lecture me on social graces?"

There was a long, hard silence as the two stood nose to nose. Then the young woman turned to the braves and women standing around the entrance and began shouting out orders in the Nez Perce tongue. Quickly responding, some began to clean out the hut, and others reassembled the steaming, burning logs to boil water outside.

"Ask some of the men to help me carefully move the chief near the door so I can see what I'm doing. When I'm done operating, we can move him back and build a smaller fire," Tom said.

Soon, the room was put right. Tom soaked his metal instruments in boiling water and then spread them out on a clean cloth to best advantage. He took a glass bottle containing a clear liquid from his wooden medical box and poured some of the contents into an atomizer. He then sprayed the instruments and the wound with the liquid and handed the atomizer to Judith. "Okay, here goes. I need several of the men to hold him down while I start probing for this bullet. It's going to smart some. Spray this liquid all over my hands while I wash them."

Tom took a deep breath, squinting his eyes, and then

carefully picked up the pair of forceps and began to probe deeply into the wound for the bullet. The chief instantly cried out in pain as Judith put a rolled-up cloth into his mouth to bite on. The young braves held him fast as Tom felt the forceps hit something hard. It was either a bone fragment or the bullet. Grasping it tightly, he eased it gently out of the wound channel and dropped it into a small metal pan with a clank. "It's a rifle bullet all right, and a big one," he said. "Looks like it came from an old army rifle—a .45-70, I'd say! I've dug these out before. It's a miracle it didn't take his arm off."

Tom scraped and debrided the wound of rancid tissue, and this time, he poured some of the clear liquid directly into the wound channel and onto the surrounding area. Patting it dry, he pressed in pieces of clean cloth and held pressure until the bleeding stopped. His patient had long passed out from the pain, but his heart beat strongly.

"I want to let this wound drain for a day or two as long as the bleeding is under control, then I might put in a few more stitches if needed to hold it together," Tom said thoughtfully. "My biggest concern is blood poisoning setting in."

Judith wiped Tom's dripping brow as he bandaged the chief's wound. "What is the purpose of that clear liquid, Doctor?" she asked with genuine curiosity in her voice. Leaning back on his haunches and wiping his bloody hands, he looked at Judith and smiled. "There is a lot we don't understand about infection, but thanks to the work of some great men of science like Pasteur and Dr. Lister, we understand that there are tiny creatures called germs that invade the wounds and cause sickness and death. They are so small that we can only see them under a microscope. If we can kill them by taking certain careful steps before, during, and after an operation, we can give the patient a better chance of survival. Dr. Lister uses carbolic acid to do this; that is what is in that clear liquid. I don't have much of it left, but when I run out, I will use whiskey instead. The alcohol in whiskey will also kill germs. It is important that the wound, the instruments, and our hands be kept clean. The chief needs to rest now to let his body take over the healing. These bandages need to be changed frequently, or we will be right back where we started. No bandages are to be reused unless they are boiled first and then air-dried. And no touching the wound area unless we spray it and our hands with the carbolic acid. Careful, though, and not too much! Don't get this stuff in your mouth or eyes. Understand?"

As Tom wiped his hands, he took a long, careful look at Judith. She was a pretty thing in spite of her frail appearance indicating that her recent past had not been healthy or happy.

"Thank you for your help; you're a good nurse," he said. "Any doctor would be glad to have you as an assistant." He was suddenly conscious that Judith might think him too familiar. She smiled back and nodded, giving no indication that she was offended. "Thank you, Doctor. Medical school has taught you well," she said. "I've never watched anything like this before."

Tom returned a humble smile. His father, constant study, and experience had taught him well—not school—but he didn't want to tell her that. Everyone believed him to be a legitimate doctor, and only Pete knew the truth. It was important that he exude confidence and skill—those were his only credentials for now.

"Can I get you anything, Doctor?" she said. Tom was tired, and as he leaned back against the wall of the sod hut, he looked at his new friend. She was intelligent and had been taught well by her parents, but it was obvious that her life here among the Indians had been fraught by hard times. She had lost a lot of weight, and her oft-mended clothes were in tatters. He wanted to ask her about her parents, but now was not the time. He would let Pete do the questioning. He was a marshal, and that was his job. "I could sure use a cup of coffee. If you could find my friend's hut over yonder, tell them that Tom would like some coffee and a cold biscuit if they have one."

Over the next few days, the men took turns sitting up with the ailing chief. He was very sick and often burned with fever. Sometimes during his fever dreams, he would call out to Chiefs Joseph and Looking Glass for help and wisdom to lead his people. He sometimes spoke in

126

surprisingly good English, and Pete could not help but think that he was a good man, mature beyond his years, sincerely loving the people in his charge and wanting only what was best for them. Then one night, perhaps in another fever dream, Pete heard him speak. "O Great Father," he began. Thinking that he was invoking the old chiefs again for their help, Pete listened intently.

"O Great Father, God of heaven and earth, I pray to You and Your Son Jesus Christ. Please heal me for Your sake and for my people's sake. But if I am to die, do not forget our treaty. I give You my trust and my whole heart—that is my part. Now, if my death is Your will, You must take me to live with You, to abide with You in Your great lodge behind the stars forever—that is Your part." Micajah's voice tapered off at the end, and he was silent. Pete checked his pulse as Tom had showed him, and it was strong. He then lay back and stared up through the smoke hole in the ceiling of the sod hut. He could see the stars and wondered what the chief had meant by his touching prayer. Pete had thought of all Indians as having their own particular religion, but this man seemed to be praying to the God of the Bible.

Well, what do you think of that? I must tell Alice when I get back, he thought as his eyes became heavy with sleep.

10
Judith Tells Her Story

Several days had passed since the chief's operation, and finally one early morning, he opened his eyes and looked about the hut. Tom had just changed his bandage, and Judith had washed him and was going to attempt to drip warm venison broth into his mouth. "I don't want him to dehydrate, and he needs to get nourishment," Tom said.

As Judith put her thumb and forefinger on the chief's chin to open his mouth, he startled her by grabbing her hand. "Tom! He's awake!" she said. Tom hurried to his side and smiled down at him. "Well, sir, you had us worried. How do you feel?" Tom asked, checking his pulse and his forehead for temperature. The chief blinked his eyes, his mind groping to understand through the mist of his broken fever. He attempted to sit up, but being very weak, he fell back quickly against his pillow. "There now, Chief. You have a long way to go before you are well enough for that. Just lay still and let Judith here feed you some broth. You remember Judith, don't you?"

Chief Micajah opened his eyes again and looked up through the smoke hole. "I never thought to see the shining sun again," he finally said in a hoarse voice. "It pleases me very much! The Great Father must have more for work for me to do." A tear escaped his eye, and he quickly sought to wipe it away with his hand. Judith took Tom by the elbow and motioned for him to turn away. The chief must not feel shame in front of a stranger. His display of emotion was a private matter. They must not intrude and would busy themselves until the chief had composed himself.

After a few moments, Tom turned again to face the chief. "My name is Thomas Brumett, but you can call me Tom. I am a doctor. I took the bullet out of your shoulder, and with the help of my friends, we stayed with you until you got better. Why don't you let Judith feed you some broth? It will make you heal faster," Tom said firmly.

The chief slowly raised his right hand and spoke. "We have much to speak of, Tom Brumett. You will stay with us until I am whole again."

"Yes, I will stay, and my friends will stay. You can meet them later. I believe you already know Arliss Moore," Tom said, helping to hold the chief up so Judith could feed him sips of broth.

The chief smiled. "Ah, yes, the buffalo soldier. I wish to see him again. He has taught me many things. He is a good friend and has helped us."

Tom smiled and spoke to Judith. "That'll do for now,"

he said, taking the broth cup from her hand. "Chief, you need to rest now. If you need anything, ask the brave guarding the door, and he will fetch us." Tom pulled the blanket up to cover the chief's bare chest and stoked the fire before leaving. The crisis seemed to be past, but he was still very weak.

As Tom and Judith walked through the snow to find Pete and Arliss, she began to stumble, and Tom caught her. "Judith, you must eat something and get some rest, or you will be sick too. Come with me and let Pete feed you one of his good meals. When was the last time you had good biscuits and milk gravy?"

Judith smiled and leaned on Tom's shoulder. "I suppose I am a funny one. Eating and sleeping are two things I do only when I must. If someone doesn't remind me to eat, I will forget." Her voice was weary. "I always counted on Mother to do that."

"Well," Tom said, "from now on you are my patient and charge, so I want you to eat on time and sleep on time. Your aunt and uncle are waiting for you back in Cantana."

"Cantana?" she asked with a grin. "What a strange name for a town. Is it in Montana or Canada?"

Tom chuckled. "Well, officially it is in Montana on the Canadian border, but you never can tell. Pete says that depending on which way the wind is blowing, it might be in either place, but if you come with us, you'll be seeing it soon enough."

* * *

It was late afternoon, and with the young chief resting comfortably, Judith took respite in the hut of her newfound friends, enjoying a slice of fried pork with golden-brown biscuits and peppery milk gravy. Pete had saved some bits of sourdough from his broken jar after the wolf mishap and already had a new jar of mother working in a warm place next to the fire. In a few days, he would be able to make tasty sourdough bread and pancakes again. Judith seemed impressed by the abilities of these strange men who had suddenly intruded into her lonely life. After eating a slice of pastry dough baked with butter and brown sugar oozing from its side, it was time for fresh coffee and questions.

Pete leaned back against the wall of the hut to address his friends as the hot, cheery fire crackled before them. "Judith, if you don't mind us asking, what happened to your folks? How did they die?"

Until that moment, Judith had not spoken much about her past or what had happened to her parents several months ago. She rested her cup on her knee, and after a thoughtful moment, she spoke. "It was about eight months ago. Some rough men came to our camp here in the mountains and asked for food and a place to bed down. There were only five or six of them, and Chief Michael wanted to be hospitable, so he fed them and let them stay in one of the huts. Sometime during the night, they turned on us and attacked us. They must have had other men hiding in the dark, because when I looked, there seemed to be more than a dozen of them. They had heard tales that Indians hoarded gold. They cruelly questioned some of the Indians, murdering some and torturing others. My father tried to intervene and reason with them, but they would have none of it. Pa had hidden me in one of the collapsed sod huts out of the way and made me promise not to come out or show myself, for he knew that if the outlaws knew I was here . . ." Judith paused to wipe a tear from her cheek.

"When the outlaws had gotten as much information as they could, they fled down the mountain. Several braves, some women and children, and my parents lay dead. Afterwards, some of the men wanted to go after them, but Michael said no, this wasn't the time. We had our wounded to care for and dead to bury and the security of the camp to think about. And Michael knew that they possessed neither the weapons nor the skills to prevail."

Judith continued her narrative. "Personally, Michael was devastated and blamed his youth and naiveté for the whole thing. The braves who brought Michael back to camp the other day after the shooting said they were sure these were the same men who attacked us months ago. We have been living in constant fear ever since. We think they might come back again and finish it because they still believe we have the gold and are hiding it. The chief knows that we are unprepared for such an attack. The braves will fight, but they are very young, untrained, and so very few. One good assault and it will be over for all of us—the end of Chief Michael's band of the Nez Perce."

"Is there gold?" Pete asked.

Judith didn't hesitate. "No! There never was any gold. When the people escaped from the battle twenty years ago, they had little time to take along the things they would need, let alone something like that—even if it had existed. The people do not care about gold and are amazed at the white man's infatuation with it. If we would have had gold when the men attacked us eight months ago, we would have gladly given it to them."

Pete gazed deeply into the firelight. "I have noticed that you call him 'Michael,'" he said.

Judith smiled. "Chief Micajah or Michael and I grew up together. He is like my older brother, and I have the privilege of calling him by that name when no one else is around. In public, though, I must address him by his proper name and title because his status as chief and leader must be preserved—for the sake of our people."

"Our people?" Pete remarked.

"I have been here, Marshal, since I was a very little girl. I love these people, and I and my parents have given our lives for their sakes. I suppose, in a way, they are my people. When my parents came here from the East, they stopped by Fort Maginnis further south of here, by the Judith Mountains where I was born. In fact, that is where I got my name. Montana and the Nez Perce people are all that I have ever known."

Pete gazed intently at Judith before speaking. "I know this may not be an easy question to answer, but do you have regard for the chief beyond what you told us . . . let's say, of a personal nature?"

Tom shot a glance at Pete, surprised at such a delicate question. But it having been asked, he wanted to know the answer too.

"No, Marshal," Judith said, staring back at Pete without emotion, blinking through the smoky firelight. "As I said, Michael is my older brother, and that is all. I love him only in that way. His woman and soon-to-be wife is Snowbird. They were to be married before this trouble and his shooting upset everything. Doctor Tom and Arliss met her when they first entered Chief Michael's hut, but they did not know who she was. Hopefully, when happier times come for the people, we can again concentrate on their marriage, and perhaps the chief will have an heir. Why did you ask me such a question?"

Pete set his cup down, and his expression was grim. "It appears that the chief is goin' to live, but he will be weak for a long time. He will listen to you, Judith, because he trusts you. I need to know if you are able to give him advice with a clear head. If we are to get out of here alive and preserve what's left of these Nez Perce, we must plan and plan well."

"Get out of here alive?" Judith responded, echoing

Pete's words. "Michael will never leave the Bear Paws! He is all that is left of the Nez Perce people who refused to sign an unfair treaty and were butchered by the army because of it. He will die here if he must!"

Pete stiffened his jaw and looked hard at young Judith Farnsworth. "Then die he must, and with him, all of those who are tender and blameless and looking to him for protection! And with their deaths goes everything you and your parents worked for. I understand why they came here twenty-some years ago, but times have changed. As our country becomes more and more civilized, this place will be discovered by more people, and then what? Already a band of murderin' thugs knows of it, and I am sure they are nearby and will be back when the snows are over in the springtime. The other Indian tribes aren't stupid either! I'm sure they know of the Nez Perce, and probably have for a long time. The chief needs to understand that to preserve his people, he must leave the Bear Paw Mountains forever and perhaps go to live with the main tribe out west. That is why you must agree to back up our talk. You have his ear, and he will honor your wisdom."

Judith's mouth dropped open, and with great emotion she spoke. "There is no tribe out west! Michael says so, and so did the old ones before they died. Young Joseph and the Nez Perce people were pursued from Oregon through Idaho, Wyoming, and then Montana by the army. They were utterly slaughtered in a vicious battle over two decades ago. They tried to get across the Medicine Line into Canada but were destroyed except for this small band that escaped here. We are all alone!"

Pete took a deep breath and turned to Arliss Moore. "Judith, you know Arliss here. He has visited and traded with the people before. You know that he was once a soldier with the army, and he knows many things that you and the chief do not. I will let him tell you."

Arliss stirred the fire with a long stick, which was his custom when he was thoughtful. "Ma'am, Chief Joseph did not die in the battle twenty years ago. He surrendered to stop the killing and preserve the lives of his people. Chief White Bird and some of his band did get away under the cover of darkness and cross the border, or the Medicine Line as you call it, into Canada. Joseph and the remnants of the main tribe were taken to Kansas and then Oklahoma by the army. Several years later they were allowed to return—some to Idaho and others to Washington State. Chief Joseph still lives and is on a reservation in Washington."

Judith Farnsworth sat back, dumbfounded, taking in a great breath of air. "Michael did not know this! He felt so alone with the great weight that had been placed upon him. Most of the chiefs had their fathers and uncles and other chiefs to teach them manhood and how to lead. Michael has had none of those advantages." Then she looked intently into the faces of the three men who sat before her. "If we must leave, then I put this to you three men who are most remarkable—a soldier, a lawman, and a doctor. You are wise, experienced, and from what I have seen, worthy men —each a man's man! You must be Chief Michael's counselors. You must teach him what you know and then lead him—lead *us* out of here to rejoin our people in the west."

Pete looked at Judith, feeling the fiery emotion and urgency of her plea. "Miss Judith, Arliss here had that same idea before we arrived. We will help the young chief if he will have us. All we ask is that you let us tell him, when we feel the time is right, that Chief Joseph and the rest of the Nez Perce still live. You must trust us on this."

"I will, Pete," she promised after some hesitation. "I will let you tell him, even though I don't understand."

Later, after Judith retired to her hut and Tom returned from checking on the chief, the three men again sat around the fire. "Well, fellows," Pete spoke. "How's about it? It looks like we are going to be snowed in until the Chinook blows. I say we offer our help to the young chief. I have some ideas, and I'll bet you do too. And somewhere out there in the dark and bitter cold are our bloodthirsty gold-seeking friends camped out in the foothills. We must find them and not allow them to get out of paying for what they have done. Let them think the Nez Perce are helpless, just sitting here waiting to be picked off like a covey of quail, but in reality—we will be after them."

Tom and Arliss both grinned and nodded at Pete.

"Well, I'm in," said Tom. "What about you, Buffalo Soldier?"

Poking the fire once more good and hard, Arliss answered. "Why not—I haven't anything else to do."

11
Sergeant LaForge

Early that morning, Marshal Brenton unlocked the door to the deserted jailhouse and walked in. The snow outside was drifting and deep, and the wind that cut at his back was bitter and sharp. The room was dark and quiet, and he could see his breath, something he hadn't yet gotten used to. Pete always had a cheery, roaring fire going in the cast-iron stove, with hot coffee boiling and the smells of something pleasant cooking for breakfast. The large kerosene lantern that hung from the ceiling would burn brightly. The marshal had always looked forward to coming to his office in the morning, but now as he looked about the dismal, lonely room, it had become a bland, tasteless chore.

More than a month had passed since he waved good-bye to his young deputy and his greenhorn companion. Every day, morning and evening, he walked out to the edge of town and stared south across the empty prairie, hoping to catch a glimpse of them and the missing Farnsworths making their way into town. His gut told him that something had happened, perhaps something tragic. He knew that he would eventually have to find out for himself, but he was all alone in this, and there was no one he could count on to go with him. He had discussed it with Melinda, preparing her for the day when he would have to set trail for the Bear Paws. That day would come soon.

Tossing several lumps of coal into the stove and dousing it with a splash of kerosene from the metal can in the corner, he struck a match against the side of the stove. He picked up the coffeepot and swished it around. It was more than half-full of coffee slush from the day before, so he decided to just to heat it up again. He had a hankering for Pete's coffee, which was actually pretty good, but Brenton would never own up to it. Teasing Pete about his coffee was something he relished, and he would be glad to have him back at his duties at the marshal's office in Cantana once more.

Later that morning through the howling of the wind, Brenton could hear a horse outside the door and quickly rose to see who it was. Had Pete finally made it back? Scurrying to open the door and look into the street, Brenton grinned. "C'mon in, Jim," he said loudly. "I was wondering if you had gone and retired without letting me know."

Quickly stepping up onto the wooden boardwalk and briskly shaking the marshal's hand was Sergeant Jim LaForge of the North-West Mounted Police, a frequent visitor to Cantana from his detachment above the Canadian border. "Let me tend to my horse first, Dave, and I'll be right in," he said. As Brenton waited, he walked his horse across the deserted street to the livery stable.

LaForge entered the jailhouse without fanfare, unbuttoning his heavy fur coat and removing his fur-trimmed hat and hanging them on the wooden pegs on the wall. He smoothed out his bright red serge tunic and adjusted the white lanyard that was fastened around his neck, securing his revolver. He was an impressive figure, thin and lean, with his bright yellow sergeant's stripes and shoulder stars showing he had been a member of the force for many years. His jet-black hair mingled with gray and carefully trimmed mustache stood out against his cold-reddened face. Bidding him to take a seat, the marshal quickly handed him a cup of hot coffee.

"What brings ya by, Jim?" the marshal asked, indeed happy for the company. "What are you doing out on a day like this? Did you fall off your horse on the wrong side of the border again?"

Sergeant LaForge smiled. "Well, Dave, actually, I'm here on crown business. The queen sent me here to run you Americans off her land. She says that Cantana is part of the dominion, and you are all squatters."

David Brenton chuckled. "You tell Her Majesty that she can have it anytime she wants it. It would be nice to be wanted by somebody. Helena doesn't seem to know we are here."

Both of the men laughed at the long-running joke between them. The Canadian border was so close that sometimes Brenton wondered if perhaps they were indeed in Canada. He surely saw more Mounties than he did US soldiers.

"Jim, how long can you stay? Melinda's roasting a ham with her famous scalloped potatoes for supper, and this is also her bread-baking day. She would love to have your company and hear some news. I hope, someday, we can meet your wife, Marta. We feel like we already know her."

Sergeant LaForge sat back in his chair and took another sip from his steaming cup. "I don't have to leave until morning, and I was hoping for an invite. I would be much obliged to break bread with you and Melinda. By the way, where's your young deputy? I'm used to seeing him making flapjacks and frying sausage."

Marshal Brenton set his cup down on his desk, and interlacing his fingers, he leaned forward, relating the whole story about the Farnsworths, Tom Brumett, and the Indians down south in the Bear Paws.

"So—what about this cheechako that Pete has with him? A help or hindrance?" Jim asked.

"A little of both, I'm afraid. I believe he is a good man—an able man as far as it goes, but he's very young and green. Pete has taken a shine to him and has high hopes," Brenton answered.

"What do you think could have happened to them,

Dave? And are you going to look for them?"

"I'm not sure what has delayed them—maybe the weather or somethin' at the Indian camp, if there be any Indians. I received word several days ago from an army scout passin' through to be on the lookout for a gang of thugs operating in this part of the state. Seems they've been terrorizing some of the Indians living in the more isolated parts of the reservations. I didn't know that before I let Pete go. Maybe they met up with these fellows. All I know is that as soon as the weather permits, I'm going to the Bear Paws."

LaForge leaned forward in his chair, holding his cup with both hands. "News travels fast, Dave. I received the same information. Evidently, they have been doing the same thing to the tribes under our protection, moving freely above and below the line. Canada would like to get a hold of them too. When do you think you might be leaving for the Bear Paws? You don't have it in your head to go it alone, do you?"

"I might be able to organize a posse by the time I have to go. Maybe one of the ranchers will let me deputize a couple of his men."

"Good men are hard to find and hang on to," LaForge said, "and ranchers usually need every able-bodied man they can hire. Besides that, not many men would leave a warm bunkhouse to follow you south into a bloody skirmish. And I don't see the prospects in Cantana as much better. Most every male in this town is either a schoolboy or in his sere and yellow."

"You're right about that, but probably not any more decrepit than an old marshal and a sergeant of the Mounties I know," Brenton said, smiling.

The two lawmen sat quietly, thinking about Pete and Tom and what could have happened to them on their mission of mercy. Finally, clearing his throat, Sergeant LaForge spoke. "Dave, you know that I am due to retire soon—this spring, as a matter of fact. I've spent the last twenty-five years bouncing back and forth between Fort Macleod and headquarters in Regina, working detachments all along the line. Now it's time to relax a little and spend some time with my good wife. She has been so patient through these long years, but I know she's grown weary of her life in Regina as a grass widow. But first, I would like to go with you to the Bear Paws if you'll have me. I could bring Marta by, and she would be good company for Melinda." Then, after a quiet pause, "I owe you a lot, Dave. Let me go with you."

Brenton said nothing but sat back in his chair, staring at his friend.

Sergeant LaForge let his mind drift back to the early days when he was only a young, inexperienced constable and the North-West Mounted Police were in their infancy. He and his partner, stationed at Fort Walsh near what would one day become the Alberta-Saskatchewan border, had been sent on the trail of a gang of men suspected of smuggling whiskey and guns to trade with the Indians. Information had been received that the outlaws had built a cabin just over the line from Montana Territory, using it as a staging point for their illegal activities. After a several days' ride across the rolling prairie, the two young Mounties decided to make camp in a deep coulee just north of the border. As they sought out a sheltered spot to build a fire near fresh water, they were not aware that they were riding into an ambush. The smugglers' cabin was just over a nearby rise, and an outlaw sentry had caught sight of them as they approached. A vicious shoot-out quickly ensued, and Jim's partner and their faithful tracking dog were killed almost instantly. LaForge managed to take refuge in the nearby underbrush and find cover at the end of the ravine, but he was pinned down and terribly outnumbered. After more than an hour of shooting, he knew the end was probably near. He could see and hear the men working their way toward him, and feeling along his cartridge belt, he realized he only had four rounds left. Determined to make every shot count, he would wait patiently and take as many with him as he could.

All alone and resigned to the outcome, he thought about the pretty girl he'd left back home in Toronto. He and Marta had grown up together, and he had loved her from the first time he met her in school. She was beautiful, with hair as shiny and black as an obsidian arrowhead and the sweet fragrance of a vanilla orchid. He wanted to ask her for her hand but was loath to do so because he had just joined up with the newly formed North-West Mounted Police. Bidding her a dismal good-bye in her parents' living room only an hour before he was to depart for Fort Dufferin in Manitoba, he was to soon begin his odyssey to the far west territories. Saddened in heart and sure that he would never see her again, he stood on the station platform, ready to join himself with the other enlisted men. He was therefore startled when he turned around and there, standing beside him, was Marta. As the train signaled its imminent departure from the station, with a hug and kiss, she assured him that she would wait for him.

Another whistling bullet slammed into the tree next to his right shoulder. He shook off his daydream and embraced the bitter reality of his situation. Carefully removing his glove to wipe the flecks of tree bark from his eyes, LaForge settled back against the side of the hill. With warm, salty sweat and dust turning to muddy streaks down his face and neck, mosquitoes and blackflies biting him without mercy, he awaited the inevitable in the stifling, motionless air.

Then, startled and wheeling about, LaForge heard a voice high above him on the creek bank. "Can anybody get in on this, or is this a private party?"

LaForge pulled back the hammer of his rifle and pointed it in the direction of the intruder's voice. "So you found me, have you? At least identify yourself and come down where I can see you—you back-shooting cowards! I order you in the name of the crown!"

"Don't shoot, my young Mountie friend. I'm Sergeant David Brenton, United States Cavalry, from the outpost in Cantana below the line. Be easy, now, and I'll show myself."

Brenton slowly and carefully made his way down the hill, holding his rifle in plain sight away from his body.

"What are you doing up here, Sergeant? Out of your jurisdiction a mite, aren't you?" LaForge asked, surprised and relieved at the same time.

"Yes, and you'd better well be glad that I am. There are several rough-looking fellows on the other end of this ravine with rifles aimed at your gizzard. Why don't you just stand up and wave a red flag at 'em and be done with it?" Brenton said, making reference to the young Mountie's bright red tunic.

LaForge didn't appreciate the humor. "What are you doing here, and how did you find me?" he asked, trying to maintain an air of authority with this American who seemed to find humor in everything. Brenton took his place next to LaForge, pointing his rifle toward the other end of the ravine. "Well, it just so happened that a couple of fur trappers from your neck of the woods came into town to trade for supplies and stopped by our outpost. They told us that a couple of redcoats were shooting it out at the smugglers' camp north of the line. I just thought I'd come up and take a closer look."

Still breathing a sigh of relief but feeling the need to register a formal protest, LaForge spoke gruffly. "See here, Sergeant Whoever-you-are, you have no authority here and will just get us both into trouble."

Brenton chuckled. "Well, son, in case you don't know it, you're already in a heap of trouble! Or do you think you're going to get a better offer of help today? Why don't you just deputize me and be done with it. Let's just say I'm a stranger who happened along, who's graciously offered his help to the queen."

"But it wouldn't be legal or right. You're an American soldier," LaForge muttered. Just then, another rifle bullet whizzed over his head. Then another shattered a tree branch near his side. Quickly hunkering down in the sand, he turned to his newfound friend. "You're deputized, Sergeant! Start shooting!"

The exchange lasted for only a few moments and suddenly stopped, as if the outlaws sensed the Mountie had somehow gotten reinforcements. Brenton looked at his younger companion. "Hold out your hand!" he said, reaching into his pocket and pulling out several boxes of rifle cartridges. "I think these should fit your rifle. You Mounties use that confounded .45-75 cartridge that nobody else around here uses, so I grabbed a couple boxes on my way out. Load up and lay down a barrage of fire to keep their heads down, and don't let up! And for goodness' sake

—don't shoot me!"

LaForge nodded as Brenton crawled back up over the hill and melted away into the brush, taking advantage of the shooting noise and smoke. After twenty minutes or so and with most of his shells gone, there was a long silence. LaForge wondered if the American had been killed.

Then he heard it—loud voices and shouting and the distant report of a rifle, further to the left of where the outlaws had been shooting. Several more rapid shots were heard, and then all was silent. Waiting for the worst possible news, LaForge loaded the last several cartridges into his rifle and tossed the empty brown paper boxes to the side. Sitting motionless, his large eyes moved rapidly from side to side. He barely was able to take a breath, the blackflies chewing at his face and hands. *It feels like liquid fire!* he thought.

"Ho, Mountie! You got a shovel?" the sergeant's voice rang out from the distance.

Constable LaForge stood up and made his way through the thick brush and cover to find the sergeant standing over the bodies of four men, each sporting a carefully placed bullet hole. LaForge glanced at Brenton and then gazed upon the lifeless faces lying on the ground before him. So these were the men who had killed his partner and faithful dog and tried to kill him—all over rotgut whiskey! These men—bold intruders from below the border—had demonstrated that they would stick at nothing and had now paid for it with their lives. He felt no pity or remorse. This was how it was out here.

"I tried to let them surrender, but they wouldn't have it that way," Brenton said, taking off his hat to fan away the ever-present biting insects. "Likely they are all Americans, so I guess it's only fittin' that I was the one to do the dirty deed. I know you Mounties don't like this sort of thing— bring 'em back alive and all that—but given half a chance, they would have killed us like they did your partner over there, so no maudlin tears need be shed on their behalf. We can bury this trash right here where they lay." The sergeant spoke harshly, touching one of the dead smugglers with the barrel of his rifle.

Brenton's words stung. "I don't know what you think you've heard about us, Sergeant, but we're just as willing and able to bring down fire upon our enemies as you are. These fellows dry-gulched us, as you Americans like to say, or it would have been our bullets in them now. We may be a police force and not the army, I know we get spread pretty thin sometimes, but we are just as capable of getting the job done!" With the hot sweat running down his insect-bitten face and his last nerve trodden upon by this chiding American, LaForge felt miserable.

"I meant no offense, Constable. When it comes to fighting outlaws, it doesn't matter in my book if it's American or Canadian lead that ends it. What do you want to do about your friend over there?" The sergeant motioning to the lifeless body of the North-West Mounted Policeman that lay crumpled in the grass. "With this heat, it's best that we get him underground as soon as we can."

LaForge, finally letting down his guard, kneeled next to the body of his friend, putting his hand upon his shoulder. Daniel had been the dear brother he never had, the Jonathan to his David. They had grown up together in the streets of Toronto, and joining the Mounties was to be the grand adventure of a lifetime for them both. LaForge was to be the best man at Daniel's wedding upon his promotion to corporal, and both had agreed to name their first sons after the other. Now he would have to write his parents and fiancée and attempt to put into words how Daniel had died bravely in the line of duty, a great waste of a fine life.

LaForge took a long, hard look at his new friend in the blue cavalry uniform and slouch hat. He had always detested Americans. The border to him was nothing more than a nuisance—a pipeline for every sort of miscreant to simply walk across into his country. But now he was genuinely grateful, and he subconsciously made a pact with himself that this man would be his friend, and he would find some way to repay him for his help this day.

Sergeant LaForge could hear the sound of David Brenton's voice pulling him back from his memories.

Smiling at him from behind his desk, Brenton spoke again. "Hey Jim, are you listening?" he asked.

LaForge smiled. "Sorry, Dave. Just remembering the

first time you and I met. Were we ever that young?"

"I'm afraid so, but that was a long time ago. As these brown spots on the backs of my hands declare."

"I haven't forgotten that I owe you my life and haven't been able to adequately repay you through these long, lonely years of our friendship," Jim said seriously.

"But you don't owe me anything, Jim. I just figured it was one lawman helping another, and not letting a little thing like an invisible line in the prairie dust get in the way of it."

Jim winked and nodded at his friend. "Thanks, Dave. And I would like to visit the cemetery before I leave tomorrow. It will probably be the last time I get to see my old friend Daniel while still wearing this uniform—you understand, of course. I'll never forget your kindness in allowing me to bury him here, and the dog too. He was a good dog, and we considered him one of us. And I will not forget the gesture, when you brought along that sack full of Canadian soil to bury with them."

"Well, it only seemed right. I saw to it that it's recorded in the town records that those two plots of earth are considered part of Canada—now and forever," the marshal said. "And, Jim, I couldn't think of anyone I would rather have at my side. You have been a good and faithful friend through the years, but I can't allow you to risk everything, not when you and your Marta are ready to start enjoying life again. I'll get someone to help me, sure enough, so don't worry about it. Now let's have no more talk of this. Let's get you settled in for the night. It's almost noon, and we are just in time for dinner. I think Melinda is heating up leftover chicken and dumplings from last night's supper. They're even better the second day."

* * *

Alice dismissed her students, and after the last of them departed the classroom that had been set up downstairs in her father's hotel, she rose to put another piece of coal into the stove so she could continue working. Sitting back down at her desk to finish grading a few papers and working on tomorrow's lessons, she put her elbow on the desk and the back of her hand under her chin to gaze out the window. Only able to occasionally discern any buildings or people through the snowing, blowing, wintry world outside, she prayed that her students living in the town limits would make it home safely. The several who lived out on the prairie, mostly farmers' and a few ranchers' kids, would stay here at the hotel until the weather moderated. Christmas was only a few days away, and one of the ranchers had brought in a pine tree for the students to decorate. Pine trees were scarce on the prairie except for high up in the mountains, but some grew them as wind breaks around their ranch houses. She looked forward to trimming the tree tomorrow and the little Christmas party they would have.

Alice looked at the corner of her desk and smiled. Several carrots, parsnips, turnips, and other assorted root vegetables lay there, reminding her that prairie teachers did not always receive apples from their students like teachers in the East, especially in the wintertime. She thought about the little cold, red faces that had brought her these tokens and realized that if the natural thing happened, all of this, her life and the lives of her students, would soon change as Cantana went away.

Finally, as the sun winked at her from between the low clouds on the cold horizon, she closed her grade book and gathered those gifts that had that very morning been in a prairie root cellar and carried them to the kitchen. Seated again in the warm drawing room of the large hotel, she sipped a cup of hot tea. She felt something touch the back of her hand and realized it was a tear that had escaped her eye as she thought about that cold morning in late November when she bade Pete good-bye with a hug and kiss. She had expected his return no later than a fortnight, but now it had been many weeks and she had no way of knowing if he was injured or even dead. She loved him, but she wasn't naïve. Pete was not comfortable coming to church, and she sort of understood that he did so just to stay in her graces and because she was the only eligible girl in town. He smiled when she spoke to him about God and only endured their conversations about spiritual matters. She knew she had to be careful and not get ahead of him. She envisioned being his wife someday, but she wouldn't marry him unless they could honestly share everything together—and that included a spiritual life. *"Can two walk together, except they be agreed?"* she remembered from the book of Amos in the Old Testament. When the newness and glow of their marriage had faded away, reality would settle upon their day-by-day lives, and Pete's unhappiness with her faith would make him feel trapped, and he would resent her. Alice loved Pete and prayed that he would become a Christian, but she would not marry him if they couldn't sincerely share Christ in their hearts and lives together.

12
Old Warhorses

As stormy waves smashed with fierceness along the Pacific coasts of Washington State and Vancouver Island and heavy rains poured hard against the western side of the Rocky Mountains, the bitter winter air from high above the peaks was driven up and pushed over to sink onto the prairies of the leeward side. As the air sank, it compressed and heated, becoming a hard wind, blowing and spilling out across the plains like a spreading blanket. The snow, many feet deep in some places, began to melt rapidly, and soon, shimmering lakes and marshes mottled the greening landscape. These were the Chinook winds that the winter-weary people of the plains so desperately awaited to give them relief and hope, to save their snowbound, starving cattle. Although the winter was not over, this brief respite provided the needed window for Marshal Brenton to search for Pete and Tom and hopefully solve the mystery of their long delay.

David Brenton took off his hat and stood out on the

prairie east of the main street, savoring the warm winds that blew through the faded yellow and brown grasses and whistled through the coulee near the edge of town. The Chinook had melted every vestige of snow, and even though the ground was soggy, the constant, driven breezes would soon dry it out. Brenton ran his fingers through his hair, and replacing his hat, resolved that he would delay no longer. He would leave in the morning for the Bear Paws.

He had not been able to get a posse together from the surrounding ranches and farms. He understood. They all had responsibilities of their own, and after they heard his story, he could tell there was little empathy for Pete and Tom's undertaking of mercy to the missionaries and the Indians. The only person offering to help was Bill Hester, the old blacksmith, who was in his seventies. David smiled and thanked him for his offer, making him acting marshal until his return.

The Farnsworths, who had started this whole affair, had long ago returned to Chicago. Weary of waiting, and with pressing business affairs and the hardships of prairie life a little more than they were able to manage, they left, giving up in resignation to their brother's fate.

The sun being low in the western sky, David Brenton locked up the jailhouse and sauntered home. Walking through the door of his storefront abode, he hung his hat and gun belt on the wall peg and stood for a moment to observe his wife who was stirring a beef stew on the stove.

Greeting her with a kiss and a loving squeeze, he took his seat in the old chair by the window.

Melinda Brenton was a tough lady and had lived through the many years of action and danger in her husband's exciting life. But this was different. He wasn't a young man anymore, and they had talked so much lately about his retirement and raising a few chickens on a small farm in Oregon. He had always been so audacious and gotten away with it, but now he would be riding perhaps fifty or sixty miles south into the mountains to unknown circumstances and danger—all by himself. She had hoped that a sympathetic rancher might send several of his men along to help, but that did not happen, and now she knew where her husband stood. All of his faithful years as their marshal did not seem to count for anything. But Melinda also understood duty. David had to go—for the sake of his badge, for the sake of Pete and Tom, and for the sake of those needing his help and protection.

That evening they spoke little during supper, but as David retired early, she held onto him and cherished him as if she would never see him again. They had not been able to have children, and all they had was each other. She loved this old lawman, and Melinda knew that if anything happened to him, she would not be able to easily forgive those who could have helped him but didn't.

Morning came early after a night of elusive and tormented sleep. Melinda hurried to stoke the fire in the stove and get breakfast ready and coffee on. She had spent the previous day preparing enough food for David to last several days and ease his burden of having to contrive meals. After her husband kissed her good morning and let his suspenders snap into place, Melinda opened the door and walked out onto the porch. Their humble house was only a converted storefront, not more than several doors down from the jailhouse, but it was home. The morning was dark but clear, and the slight breeze chilly. The stars were bright, and there was no sign of the impending sun.

As Melinda crossed her arms, pulling her shawl tightly about her shoulders, she could hear several horses coming down the deserted main street in the shadows. As the horses approached, she could make out two riders. The one in front appeared to be a woman wrapped securely in a buffalo robe. As the horses pulled up to the hitching rail before her, she immediately recognized the second rider.

"Ho in the house! I hear tell that it's possible to get coffee and breakfast at this fine establishment. Is that true?" the rider shouted out, dismounting his horse and helping the female rider down. Melinda knew that voice well!

"David! Bring the lantern and come quickly!" she shouted through the doorway. Holding the lantern high, David laughed out loud as the yellow light caught the unmistakable hat of a North-West Mounted Policeman. It was their old friend Sergeant Jim LaForge.

"Jim! What a surprise! And is this who I think it is?"

David asked, shaking the Mountie's hand.

"Folks, I want you to meet my dear wife Marta, fresh from cantonment in Regina." Melinda held out her hand to Marta, and then pausing, she hurried to embrace her. "After all of these years with Jim's visits and him speaking of you, I feel that I know you well. Come in out of this chill," she said.

Seated around the table, enjoying a breakfast of pancakes and sausage and eggs, the Brentons and the LaForges chatted cheerfully, not mindful of the time. But soon, the glow from the eastern sky became visible through the large storefront window. Suddenly brought back to reality, David set down his coffee cup, wiped his mouth with a cloth napkin, and looked at his guests. "Jim, I'm sorry that I won't be able to stay and visit. You caught me on my way out. I must be going in a few moments to find Pete and Tom, and I don't know how long this good weather might last," he said soberly. "Marta here must think I'm powerful rude."

"Well, Dave, this isn't just a social call for me either. I was hoping that Marta could stay with Melinda for a while so I can accompany you down there. It seems those outlaws we talked about are now officially wanted in Canada. I have warrants from my government," Jim said, reaching into his tunic and pulling out a fistful of papers. "I have been given permission by my inspector, sort of on the quiet, of course, to go after them wherever I may find them. His gift to me on the heels of my retirement. If you'll allow me, I'd like to go along with you. I figure an old Mountie and a retired cavalry sergeant should be about equal to anything that comes along. I think we can make quick work of them and bring them to justice. What do you say?"

Unable to contain herself, Melinda stood up and rushed over to Jim, giving him a hug. "Oh, Jim, you don't know what this means to me—to *us!* David couldn't find anybody to help him. Oh, thank you, thank you so much! And yes—I would love to have Marta stay with me, as long as she likes!"

David grinned and said, "Jim, raise your right hand. Do you swear to perform the duties of a deputy marshal?"

"I do," LaForge answered with his right hand in the air.

"Then by the authority vested in me as marshal of the town of Cantana, Choteau County, State of Montana, I authorize you to accompany me to find these outlaws and bring them to justice."

David and Jim quickly stood up, heartily shaking each other's hands. "Then let's get going," David said. "I should have enough grub and supplies to last for the both of us."

* * *

The days and weeks passed swiftly in the camp of the Nez Perce as the young chief recovered from his wound and was able to walk about on his own. Chief Micajah or Michael regularly met with the three men to discuss the band's future. They discussed all of the possible options, including a suggestion from Pete that he lead his people to one of the nearby Indian reservations and request sanctuary there. Michael balked emphatically, refusing to have anything to do with the other tribes who had served as scouts for the army against the Nez Perce. He especially held contempt for the Crow, whom he blamed for failing to help the Nez Perce some decades before. "Someday I may forgive their betrayal, but the people must find it within themselves to forgive for themselves," he said, shaking his head. "With this, my heart is still bad!"

Unable to persuade the chief to make what they saw as a wise, sensible decision, a move less strenuous on the young, weak, and infirm, they decided it was time to reveal to him the true story of what had happened to Chief Joseph and the rest of his tribe. At first, Michael was angry that this information had been kept from him, but when Arliss explained that they had waited until the chief was well, able to think clearly and lead his people wisely, his countenance changed. He was determined to go to them as soon as the snow melted. Michael beseeched the three men even more emphatically to help him prepare his people to make the journey.

Tom, with the help of his friend Judith Farnsworth, had set up a small hospital in one of the larger deserted sod huts, to treat the sick and determine everyone's general health. Working beside each other day after day, Tom and Judith became closer, and their friendship and mutual respect for one another grew. One particular day, after having delivered two babies in their little hospital, Judith stood back and looked at Tom with deep respect. She was impressed that someone so youthful knew so much and had resolved to learn all she could from him about medicine. If she was to accompany the band to Washington State, she needed every skill she could acquire.

Tom enjoyed Judith's company, and though she had been isolated here among the Indians since her childhood, her parents had educated her well. Her conversation and vocabulary sparkled, and they began to take walks together when the work was caught up. He didn't want to admit that he had feelings for her, especially since they would be parting ways soon. The less involved he became the better. Besides, her heart was obviously set on carrying on her parents' work, and that didn't include anyone else — especially a young, spurious doctor.

When the refugees who were to one day become Michael's band of Nez Perce had escaped during and after the battle where so many of the old ones had died many years ago, it seemed that a vital link to some of the knowledge and original skills of the people was broken. It would be up to Pete and Arliss to try to fill in the gaps. And not only would it be necessary for the tribe to be healthy before they could move, but that sufficient food and shelter be prepared for the long journey. They could not count on the army for supplies. Pete and Arliss would have to hunt for venison and antelope to be made into jerky to supplement what the people would be able to hunt and forage for on the way. The hides were needed for clothing and shelter and leather for moccasins. Fish were fairly abundant in the mountain streams, but there was no salt available for curing. Pete and Arliss would build a smokehouse and teach the people how to smoke meat as an alternate method of preservation to drying and salting.

The tribe's security was also a big issue, and Pete and Arliss were always wary that the outlaws could return at any time, at any moment hoping to catch them at their most vulnerable. Arliss had promised the Nez Perce that Pete would bring the men to justice, and they must keep their pledge. No one wanted to put it into words, but it was inevitable that there would be a fight. How best to accomplish that, and then afterward pull up stakes and set out for the state of Washington, was another matter.

Arliss, the former soldier and most experienced, carefully reconnoitered the area, training sentries and posting them to cover all trails leading into the mountain camp. Pete and Arliss were not surprised to find that the Nez Perce had no modern weapons. A few rusty, unserviceable rifles remained from the old days, all of the ammunition having been spent years ago. The tribe had reverted back to its native skills of using bows and arrows and spears, knives and clubs. That would have to do.

Arliss thought on the words that young Chief Michael had spoken to him: *"The old ones are gone, and we have been in hiding so long that we have forgotten how to make war."* It would be his and Pete's job to refresh the young men's skills as warriors, and perhaps teach them some things about the way the white men fight, to ensure their survival. They would begin immediately and use what they had as weapons. He would endeavor to teach them that being smart was often more important than being strong, making the brain the most effective weapon of all.

* * *

The midafternoon was bright and balmy, and knowing that the delightful Montana springtime weather could change in a moment, Melinda Brenton invited Alice to enjoy it over tea. As she approached along the boardwalk from Granfield house, Melinda and Marta stood up from their chairs in front of the old storefront to greet her.

"Alice, I want you to meet Marta LaForge. Her husband is Sergeant Jim LaForge, the Mountie who went with David to the mountains. Marta, this is Alice Granfield. She is our schoolteacher, and her folks own and run Granfield House, the town's hotel and dining establishment. She's sort of sweet on Peter Randers, David's deputy."

"Melinda, please!" Alice exclaimed, her blushing face

standing out against her white dress. "You're embarrassing me!"

"Look, honey," Marta LaForge said with a smile, "we have all had our beaus. That's how you end up old married women like us!"

"Let's sit down to tea. We can have a nice chat and enjoy the sunshine and warm breezes while they last," Melinda said. "And Marta, you must tell us all about life in Canada and the big city of Regina. I'm sure that Cantana must be quite a change and letdown from what you're used to."

"Ladies," Marta said, "Cantana is a lovely town and so peaceful, and you don't know how wonderful it is to have the quiet company of other women again. I have spent the last twenty-five years living in detachments all over the west. Ofttimes our lodgings were just little two-roomed cabins with an improvised jail cell made of two-by-fours. Jim was always gone, it seems—the only law within hundreds of miles. And for the mounted policeman, his only deputy is often his wife. I was cook, nurse, and jailer; counselor and comrade. When our son Daniel was born, Jim was off tracking a pair of brothers wanted for murder. We thought that when he was made sergeant and we went to live in Regina, life would be steady and normal, but he was gone almost as much. We finally realized that it would always be that way, and we would have to wait until his retirement to see more of each other. It's just a secret

169

between us, but Jim has often expressed a desire to explore America someday, and except for Daniel, who just joined the force, I think he would do it. Jim doesn't make close friends easily, but I believe your husband David must be his best friend. He talks about him all the time."

Marta LaForge took a sip of tea and held the cup and saucer daintily in both hands on her lap. She was a beautiful woman, with strands of gray in her raven-black hair, and not a bit shy. It was obvious that she was thoroughly enjoying her visit.

"David has always said that Canada is not so much different than America, especially up here near the border. It's just an act of God, or perhaps an error of man, that the line was drawn where it is, and the way our husbands go back and forth, you would think it not even there," Melinda said.

Marta spoke. "Well, ladies, I just want us to become good friends. We all have a stake in it, as our husbands, and boyfriends," she said, smiling and winking at Alice, "are all in this together and of the same calling. We can surely be of great comfort to each other."

* * *

"They're there, Pete, right where I didn't expect them to be," Arliss said, exhilarated in a grim sort of way. After several weeks of combing the mountains, Arliss and his handpicked braves had finally located the camp of the men suspected of committing the murderous attack on the Nez Perce many months ago and of shooting Chief Michael. "No wonder we couldn't find them. I was expecting them to be tucked in, snug in the mountains, but they fooled me. They are in a well-sheltered coulee about three miles south of here and situated against an almost sheer rock wall, giving them a three-sided view of anyone approaching. That will make it difficult to get at them, but I have some ideas. They appear to be well stocked with provisions and horses and plenty of fresh water nearby. And they have plenty of rifles, all look like Winchesters. I counted twenty-two men—real nasty-looking fellows! No wonder these young Nez Perce were overwhelmed. We are going to have to plan this one well, Pete." Arliss picked up a stick to do his fire stoking.

Pete and Arliss were alone in the hut. "Arliss, I'd like to keep Tom out of this if we can. He has a warrior's heart, but not the skills or experience. Besides, he is more valuable to everyone as a doctor, and we'll need him if this goes badly. You and I have been workin' with these braves for some time now, and they have learned fast, but none of them have ever had to kill a man. Except for our rifles, the only weapons they will have are bows and arrows and their knives and clubs for close-in fighting. Let's make our plans, and then we can sit down with the chief and lay it out for him." Arliss and Pete were quiet as they listened to the fire crackle, thinking.

171

"We could send for the army," Pete suggested after a few moments of contemplation. "Probably the smartest move. Or we could see if one of the other tribes would help us."

Arliss shook his head. "Chief Michael wants us to let his men do the job no matter what the outcome, and he fears the army and doesn't trust the other tribes, especially the Crow for helping the army against them in '77. He believes that many of his men will be future leaders of the Nez Perce people, and they need to participate in this battle. I don't know but that I have to agree with him."

Arliss took a drink of coffee. "The air is warming and the snow melting fast. We need to attack within the next several days, no more than a week at the most or they might move on—or worse, they might come back looking for us before we are ready. They know where we are but are not aware that we have found *them!* They are not going to let us take them alive, not that it is really a concern to me. These men have butchered a lot of people, including women and children. They will keep on and do more killing if we let them."

Then Arliss looked into Pete's eyes, flickering with flames from the hot fire. "It all stops here, Pete. They die or we die—there will be no in-between."

* * *

"Strangers come!" the young warrior exclaimed to Pete and Arliss as they finished breakfast in their hut. Arliss threw down his plate and rushed to the door with Pete at his heels. "Where?" he asked as the young man motioned for them to follow him. Pete smiled—the weeks of hard training were paying off and the men were sharp. Arliss had taught the young warriors well, and no man would be allowed to approach the camp unseen.

Climbing up onto a high place, the warrior pointed north. In the slowly growing dawn, Pete and Arliss could barely see two riders on horseback leading a pack mule behind them, making their way through the hills as they themselves had done months ago. Looking up ahead, Arliss motioned for the sentries to make ready to shoot their arrows down upon the strangers at his command.

"Wait, Arliss, I think I know these men—let them approach," Pete said, squinting his eyes in the poor light. Finally, the men were within a hundred yards, and Pete stood up with a grin. "It's Marshal Brenton and Sergeant LaForge! Well, I'll be a scalded cat!" he exclaimed, rushing down to meet them.

Brenton raised his hand in recognition and dismounted his horse. Pete rushed to shake his hand and that of Sergeant LaForge. "Is the coffee still hot?" David Brenton asked.

"Well, you fellows found us! We thought we were pretty well hidden."

"You covered your tracks pretty good, young man, but don't forget, I used to do this for a livin'. Anyway, I had a fair idea where you'd be from the Farnsworths' letter. We saw what was left of those wolf carcasses, and not finding your bones, I figured you couldn't be far. I could also see that you had taken on the company of a third person. I found his soddy back a ways and figured he was a friend and not a foe."

"Marshal," Pete said, "I want you to meet Arliss Moore, who saved our hides during that wolf attack. He is a retired scout and buffalo soldier from Fort Assiniboine."

Marshal Brenton shook Moore's hand and looked at him curiously. "I know you, Moore—from the old days. Can you still make those berry pies that the guys would sell their grandmothers for?"

"You remember that?" Arliss responded with a chuckle. "Well, I'll be . . ."

"And this is Sergeant Jim LaForge of the North-West Mounted Police and one of my best friends. He came along to get a closer look. Where is Tom Brumett?"

"Well, Marshal, he's busy tending his hospital in the Indian camp with his pretty assistant, Judith Farnsworth. Her parents were the missionaries we came to fetch, but sadly, they are both dead. Let's get back to the camp, and I'll explain it all to you. You gentlemen showed up just in time to help. We're cookin' up a little war for some outlaws camped over the way."

174

13
How to Make War

It was early morning in the camp of the Nez Perce, and all of the principals gathered in the council hut with Chief Michael. This would be the final meeting before the attack on the outlaws who were camped in presumed security and confidence several miles away on the edge of the prairie. It was a rare setting, with everyone there having something special to offer: Arliss Moore, the scout and buffalo soldier; Pete Randers, deputy marshal, trained to survive the harshness of the trail by his father; Tom Brumett, the young doctor; and Judith Farnsworth, missionary and nurse; David Brenton, the tough, weathered old marshal; and Sergeant Jim LaForge of the North-West Mounted Police. They were there to advise the young chief and encourage him, to discuss the final plans for the fight that must come that very night. Although no one wanted to admit it openly, they were there to settle accounts with the outlaws who had tortured and murdered the innocents among this remnant of peace-loving people who only wanted to be left alone.

When this was over and Michael's band was safely at Colville, unarmed and reduced to essentially an agrarian lifestyle forever, they needed to know in their hearts that one last time they had shed blood in a righteous cause against their enemies, defending themselves as a people.

Arliss had insisted that until this was over, all braves were to be addressed to their faces and among the people as "warriors." "If you call them warriors they will act like warriors," he said. Had he and Pete done their jobs well? That would shortly be revealed. What they had in store for the outlaws would be unleashed upon them before the next sunrise.

Chief Michael was completely healed and anxious to fight. Pete and Arliss had worked with him that long winter and counseled him on his martial and leadership skills. He would purposely be at the forefront of the battle, not only to give him confidence but to gain him the admiration and respect of his people. Pete and Arliss were hopeful that Michael's band of the Nez Perce once again knew how "to make war."

In the bright glow of a wide shaft of sunlight that shone through the opening in the roof of the large sod council hut, a space had been cleared in the center of the floor. Arliss stood up, holding a long, straight stick as a pointer, and began to speak.

"Chief and all here, let's rehearse one more time our final plan, and then we will go over it again with each and every warrior so there are no mistakes." Arliss and Pete had drilled the Nez Perce warriors for days in an open meadow, walking them through each part of the battle as it was expected to go. They had been impressed by their abilities and eagerness to learn. Now the time had come to act, and standing before an image of where the fight was to take place, Arliss pointed to the features with his stick.

"This is the camp of the outlaws. We spread a wide berth for weeks searching for it but couldn't locate it. Finally, one of our warriors spotted it, nestled in a small, three-sided coulee with a rock overhang for protection, almost like a cave—dry and out of the wind with plenty of fresh water nearby. Notice, at first, that it is almost impossible to approach them without being seen, because with their backs to this rock wall, they have a view all around them in all directions. It would take hundreds of men to attack them this way, and many would die. It would be almost impossible to get at them or get them out, like a tick in the neck of a mountain sheep. We must do something different. We had to discover the outlaws' weakness and what it was that would draw them out of camp and make them vulnerable.

"Day by day and through each night, we watched everything they did, looking for that one thing until we finally hit upon it. We noticed that their horses, about thirty or so, were tied up in a remuda sheltered under a rock overhang several hundred yards further down from their camp. The outlaws seemed to obsess about caring for them, leading them every day to water and to feed on prairie hay and from sacks of grain loaded on several wagons. I figured the only thing that would lure them out of their camp would be if they had to save their horses. To lose their horses would make them almost helpless. This was their weakness! If we could take their horses in the middle of the night, making a lot of noise and hoopla with lit torches and shouting, we could pull them out of their hole, ambush them, and then move into their camp from behind.

"Although I never attended the military school at West Point, of course, I remember one of the officers telling about this tactic. It came from the Bible, when Joshua lured the people of Ai out of their fortified city, ambushed them, and then had soldiers waiting to move into the city from behind. This outlaw's camp will be our Ai."

Arliss pointed with his stick. "Take careful notice of your positions in regard to everyone else. Chief Micajah and Pete will lead the first group of warriors, Marshal Brenton and Sergeant LaForge will lead the second group, and I will lead the third. Doc? You and Judith will set up your hospital here and be ready to treat the wounded."

Brenton smiled and nodded his head. "I think the army was crazy for letting you go, Arliss. You should have been an officer."

Pete looked on the former buffalo soldier and his friend with a new respect. He gave his briefing as well as any general might. *How could anyone treat a man like this with disrespect or keep him down when he has so much to offer?* he thought.

When the briefing was over, Chief Michael rose to his feet, and all were silent. He was young and handsome and possessed an inner, quiet wisdom that Pete and Arliss had noticed early on. He wore the traditional buckskin clothing of his people, except for a yellow cavalry scarf that Arliss had given him as a gift. He held up his hand to signal that he was about to speak.

"My friends, when the sun rises in the morning, we may not all be here together again like this. It has been a long, hard winter, and now we fight for what is right so that the memories of those who had their lives taken from them may be less bitter to us. Soon, my people will be reunited with the people in the West. Unspeakable joy fills my heart in thinking that perhaps I may see the great Chief Joseph and sit and rest at his feet. I thank you all, my friends. I will never forget you, wherever our paths may lead. Your hearts are right as my heart is right. May the Great Father and His Son Jesus, who awaits in His great lodge behind the stars, keep you all."

Again and again that afternoon and on into the evening, the plan was studied and repeated until each and every one, including every young warrior, understood his part with no mistakes. Meanwhile, Tom and Judith loaded up one of the pack mules with everything they would need

179

to set up a primitive triage and field hospital. Several of the Nez Perce women whom they had trained would be coming along to help.

Arliss admonished the warriors not to pick up any of the rifles from the felled outlaws. "I know it will be tempting, but you have not been trained to use them. Use what you know—your bows and knifes. Perhaps later on I will train you to use a rifle." Arliss knew that this would probably never happen. The Nez Perce would be going to the reservation at Colville. Somewhere along the line the army would be involved, and the people would be disarmed and not allowed to have firearms. But he did not want to dishearten the men by telling them this before the fight. When this was all over, he would speak to them about it and encourage them. He would remind them that manhood, which the Nez Perce call *simiakia*, and duty were more than just having a rifle.

Arliss had several of the warriors watching the camp of the outlaws at all times. They were told to observe the camp for about two hours and then report back as soon as they were relieved by several fresh men. This rotation gave every one of the warriors a chance to observe the ground where they were to fight and to become familiar with the route back to camp. There would be no torches, only starlight, and they would be responsible to lead everyone to the right place through the darkness and gloom. Once they started, there would be no turning back. The moon was expected to rise sometime after midnight, and the moonshine off their faces could be seen for quite a distance. If they were not in position, a surprise attack would be almost impossible. Wind direction would also be of concern. If the outlaws' horses smelled them coming, they might alert their owners with the sounds of their uneasiness.

The sun had finally set, and the men were waiting. A sort of electricity ran through them all as they watched Arliss for his signal. The stars began to appear, becoming visible in the darker, eastern sky, and the light from the sunset dimming to a mild, fading glow.

Arliss stood and held up his hand for a brief moment and then let it drop, signaling that it was time to go. Every man knew his job and where he should be, and they rapidly began to fall into place. Each groups joined upon its particular leader, and soon the long trek to the outlaw camp began.

Arliss, an experienced fighter himself, had worked hard to train these young Indian warriors who had been lost to their people and to the world for over twenty years. They had to be taught to make war for this one battle, probably never to have occasion to use those skills again. But it would give them a proud and hearty tale to tell their children and grandchildren and would form a pool of rare men from which the future leaders of the tribe might be chosen. As he trudged along at the head of the single file

181

column, Arliss took mastery of his feelings, knowing that perhaps, after this night, only a few of them would be coming back.

As the men neared the outlaw campsite, they were met by one of the warriors standing his watch. Arliss raised his arm as a signal for everyone to quietly lie low and for the leaders to join him. Pete and Chief Michael approached, with Marshal Brenton and Sergeant LaForge following close behind.

As the five men quietly drew near the camp for a closer look, the light and sparks from several campfires could be seen flickering along the rock wall. Gentle laughter mixed with the buzzing of conversation among the men, and the metallic clanking of coffee cups, plates, and utensils could be heard. Someone was playing his harmonica, which completed the pleasant setting. If one didn't know better, this camp might be mistaken for that of good, hardworking men on a legitimate cattle drive instead of a nest of murderous thugs. The lackadaisical attitude of the camp displayed the outlaws' confidence in their security—and as a further display of their arrogance, only one sleepy sentry on horseback was posted. Arliss was pleased because this would only make the surprise attack more effective. Glancing over at Pete, Chief Michael, the marshal, and Sergeant LaForge, Arliss carefully motioned for the men to rejoin the other warriors.

Arliss's plan was to begin the attack after the outlaws

had bedded down for the night, to catch them at their most vulnerable. Their horses would not be saddled, the light from the campfires dimming, and the weary men, removed of their boots, would be at ease in their bedrolls. But as Arliss knelt in contemplation at the head of the column, his whole body shuddered as he noticed a bright glow along the eastern edge of the mountains. It was the moon! Had his calculations been wrong? The moon should not be due to rise until well past midnight, but there it was, and soon it would break over the mountaintops and in the clear, cold Montana night, would make the prairie awash with its brilliance.

Arliss quickly turned to Pete and the other leaders, motioning to them to join him in a huddle. "I was off on my calculations. All I had was an old almanac to go by. The moon is rising earlier than I predicted, and we'll soon be lit up like a frosted hayfield! We need to get going now! I will take my men to the far side of the camp near the horses. Give me about twenty minutes before you move, and then Chief Micajah and Pete, you take your men and get into position on the left side. Be ready to light your fire arrows as soon as you take the camp, and when you hear me start my commotion with the horses, take the sentry out as quickly and quietly as possible and move into the camp as the outlaws pursue after us. Marshal and Sarge, when you see the fire arrows in the air, quickly move your men to the front of the camp and be in position to ambush the outlaws

183

as they find themselves caught in the middle. This will go really fast once it starts so be alert and ready. Godspeed!"

Arliss and his warriors moved swiftly and silently along the ground, making every effort to stay in any low spot they encountered that would afford them cover. Their group had the farthest to go, and their actions would begin the chain of events that would trigger the start of the battle. As they approached the horses, Arliss could hear their uneasy breathing and sounds as their sharp ears pricked, detecting his approach. Raising his hand, he signaled his warriors to stop. He would wait here to give the other two teams time to get into position.

Pete glanced at his pocket watch and then gazed over his shoulder at the fire-like glow near the summit of the Bear Paws. There was the moon, only moments away from spilling its shine on to the prairie below. He motioned for Michael and his men to move. They had to beat the moon and get into position before Arliss and his warriors began to agitate the horses.

Arliss looked at his watch. There was still five minutes to go, but he could wait no longer. He motioned to his men, and they stood up and ran to the horses, quickly cutting the ropes and slapping them hard on their backsides. Whooping and hollering, they chased the horses away from the camp, making as much noise and commotion as possible.

Several torches were lit. The outlaw camp was all astir.

The men tumbled out of their bedrolls, pulling on their boots and grabbing their Winchesters, shouting to one another as they rushed toward the direction of the horses. Pete and Chief Michael were up on their feet, and followed by their warriors, they hurried into the camp and began to ignite fire arrows, launching them high in the direction of the pursuing outlaws. Pete began to fire his rifle, making every shot count as the warriors ran for cover at the edge of the coulee, firing their arrows as fast as they were able.

The outlaws had come out of their camp about a hundred yards when Arliss whistled loudly to signal his men to stop, turn, and attack. Caught in the middle between the men in the camp and the fleeing horses, confused and in shock, the outlaws began to fire their weapons wildly in all directions as bullets skidded along the prairie grass, some striking the rock wall.

Marshal Brenton and Sergeant LaForge motioned for their warriors to follow them as they began their ambush. Not wanting the outlaws to get organized and regain their composure, Brenton and LaForge began to fire their weapons as their warriors rained down arrows. Receiving fire from three directions, the outlaws that were not dead or wounded threw down their arms and surrendered.

Arliss had been right. The battle had gone quickly once it started. It lasted less than a half-hour, and with the moon large and bright, it was time for Tom and Judith to go to work.

185

* * *

The morning's light shone from the east over the misty tops of the Bear Paw Mountains, illuminating the gun smoke that hung in the lifting shadows like rings of ghosts. The battlefield smells, the reports of rifle blasts, and the sounds of men crying out in pain as they were wounded still lingered in Pete's brain. He stood in the stillness, surveying the motionless lumps of humanity that dotted the matted grasses of the Montana springtime prairie. The thuds of shovels, piercing and stabbing the heavy sod, indicated the work of a hastily organized burial detail.

Tom and Judith, with their bloodstained clothing, were finishing up their attentions to the warriors and the several outlaws who had survived the injuries sustained in the midnight battle. Some with bruises and cuts and arrow wounds, others with severe contusions from well-placed rifle butts and clubs, and others with bullet holes and spear wounds—one resulting in an amputated leg.

Pete did a head count. Only seven of the twenty-two outlaws would be heading to Fort Assiniboine for trial and possible hanging. Two of Chief Michael's young warriors had not survived and would be carried back to the camp, to be laid to rest in the graveyard in the mountains. Marshal Brenton and Sergeant LaForge both had minor wounds from the initial spray of bullets fired by the pursuing outlaws, but they were not serious. All in all, the outcome of the skirmish was better than they could have hoped for.

The fight had been successful, and though many of the outlaws lay dead, this reckoning was necessary—that evil men learn there is a price to pay for their actions, and that sometimes that price must be paid in blood. But even on this battlefield of death, there was some comfort and satisfaction in knowing that the settlers and Indians in north-central Montana and the Canadian dominion north of the border would be safe from this latest bunch of cutthroats—at least for a while.

With the more grisly aspects of the day's deeds cared for, they would allow for a few days' rest for the wounded, and then it would be time to leave the camp in the Bear Paw Mountains forever. It had been decided that everyone would accompany Chief Michael and his band to Fort Assiniboine with the prisoners and then obtain permission from the army to allow the Nez Perce to go as far west as they were able on the railroad toward Washington State and then to Colville. Judith Farnsworth and Tom Brumett would care for the wounded as far as the fort, and then Judith would board the train going east from Havre. She had decided to make the journey to Chicago and try to get to know her uncle and aunt. Judith was very young and inexperienced in life outside the Indian camp, and without her parents to guide her, it was only appropriate for her to return to her only living relatives.

"I have decided that my parents are to stay here in the

187

mountains," she confided in Tom. "They gave their lives to the Nez Perce and died with them. I will not allow their bodies to be dug up and shipped back east like so much freight, regardless of what my uncle wants. I don't think he really ever understood my father. I'll probably live with them until I can sort out my life and find out what God wants me to do."

On the third day after the fight, everyone was packed and ready to leave. There were plenty of horses for the weak and infirm to ride, thanks to the outlaws. Chief Michael's band of Nez Perce led the column, followed by the wounded. The spoils confiscated at the outlaw camp added to their own carefully prepared provisions, and with the moderate spring weather, it would make the trek to the fort less taxing. As Pete followed up the rear, guarding the retreat, he smiled and thought that this mixed entourage to Fort Assinniboine would have been amusing if not for the bloodshed that had made it necessary. The fight was over, and now to the future.

Pete and Arliss made Michael promise that none of the people would take scalps. This would only cause trouble with the army and bring up bad feelings from the old days. However, Arliss secretly looked the other way when some of the warriors snipped a few locks of hair from the dead outlaws as mementos of the fight.

These would serve as tokens to go along with the stories the warriors would tell to their children and grandchildren.

14
Fort Assiniboine

Arliss didn't know what to expect when he arrived at Fort Assiniboine. It had been several years since he saw it last, and it had been built up considerably since then. The town of Havre just northeast of it was also growing, an indication that civilization had come to this part of the fledgling state of Montana. He located the headquarters building on the busy camp by its tall, fluttering flag. Everything seemed to come to a standstill as the soldiers stopped their duties to stare at the curious sight before them. Pete dismounted first, taking his rifle from its saddle boot to guard the prisoners. Accompanied by Marshal Brenton and Sergeant LaForge, Arliss walked up the steps and entered the doorway. "I hope this goes well," Arliss said to his companions, slapping his hat against his thigh several times to remove the dust. "It's been a long time since I was here, and I don't recognize any of these men."

Walking up to the desk outside the commanding general's office, Arliss addressed his aide-de-camp, a young officer who looked up at this giant of a man who stood before him. "I and my friends would like to see the commander. We are here with some prisoners, what's left of those whiskey and gunrunners who have been terrorizing the Indians down here and above the border."

The officer said nothing, but quickly stood up and knocked at the general's office door and disappeared inside. Within several moments, they were standing before the general to explain their unceremonious coming.

"Arliss Moore!" the general said, taking his cigar from his mouth and standing to shake his hand. "How long has it been?"

"A few years, sir," Arliss answered, returning the gesture.

"You were in the 10th under Lieutenant Pershing, if I remember correctly. Have you come back to reenlist?" The general smiled and seemed genuinely pleased to see the old buffalo soldier.

"No sir, but we have a report to make and some prisoners to bring you. We also need your help on another matter." The general bid the men before him to be seated, shouting out to his aide to bring coffee. "Now what is this all about? I am especially curious how this involves a sergeant of the North-West Mounted Police!" The general puffed on his cigar. "And *you*, Marshal! Don't I know you?"

* * *

Several days later, while awaiting the general's decision on what to do about Chief Michael and the Nez Perce, a large explosion was heard about a quarter mile out of camp. Accompanying the soldiers who rushed to investigate, Pete and the men discovered that a detail of soldiers had been blowing up tree stumps with dynamite to clear off a place for new barracks, and some of the men had been injured. Tom Brumett, who had come along, immediately went to work, helping the wounded men. This did not escape the notice of the army surgeon in charge, as Tom helped in setting broken bones, stitching up lacerations, and removing splinters of wood.

"The general wants to see all of you men," the aide said to Pete and Arliss later that evening after supper. "Oh, and he also wants to see that young doctor."

Pete, Arliss, Marshal Brenton and Sergeant LaForge entered the general's office and took a seat. Tom stood inconspicuously at the back of the room.

"Gentlemen," the general began. "I just received a telegraph message from my superiors, and after much knocking about, they gave me permission to handle the situation with the Nez Perce as I see fit. I could keep them here and make them settle on a local reservation, but I want to do what's right, so here is what I've decided to do. Arliss Moore, I would like you to accompany the Nez Perce to the Colville Reservation in Washington. You will be sworn in with the temporary rank of first sergeant. This will give you all the authority you need to complete your mission. I will send several men with you as far as the railroad will go. The authorities at the reservation know you are coming. Is that agreeable?"

Arliss smiled and nodded. "Yes sir, it is."

"And, First Sergeant Moore," the general said with a wink, "if you decide you want to come back and join us again, those stripes will be yours to keep!"

Now facing Sergeant LaForge, the general leaned back in his chair. "Sergeant, I have had communications with your government, and they have agreed to release any holds they may have on the prisoners and allow us to prosecute them here. I have wired your inspector in Regina and reported your feats. Your brave work here is done, and I thank you." The general reached across his desk to shake LaForge's hand. "I have made it part of the official record that I authorized you to take part in this mission, just in case any questions are asked about a Canadian Mountie being in Montana. I understand that the missionary girl, Miss Farnsworth, will be returned to Chicago to live with her family. I have asked several of the officers' wives to see to her clothing and other needs. Marshal Brenton, you and your deputy, no doubt, will be returning to Cantana. What a wild place that was back in the day when I made visits to our detachment there! I expect that's where I know you from. I wish you well, all of you, and I thank you for what you have done. Your story is a remarkable one."

Puffing on his cigar and lacing his fingers together across his lap, the general was thoughtful. "And you, young Doctor Brumett, I hear you are on your way to Michigan to go to medical school. Is that true?"

Tom had been leaning against the wall in the back of the room, but he came to attention, surprised that the general had addressed him particularly. "Yes . . . yes, sir!" he responded.

"Well, Doctor Brumett, I have a proposition for you. I am short a doctor, you see, and replacements are not so easy to obtain out here. The surgeon was impressed with what he saw this morning after the explosion. You seem to know your way around a surgeon's knife. If you are willing to enlist—for, say, two years—I will make you a second lieutenant, and at the end of that time, I will see you are certified as a qualified surgeon. You will get practical experience working with good doctors and will be serving your country as well. What do you say?"

Tom was stunned. He couldn't believe what he was hearing. He would be able to get his doctor's certification and not be so very far from his parents in Idaho. "Sir, I have my answer—when do I begin?" he said, still trying to let the general's words sink in.

"Captain!" the general shouted to his aide seated outside his office. "Get Lieutenant Brumett signed up and sworn in, and show him to his quarters. Good luck to you, Mr. Brumett, I look forward to having you work for me."

The general shook his hand.

"I will see you men before you go," Tom said solemnly as he smiled at his friends with whom he had had the greatest adventure of his life.

The general faced Marshal Brenton and Sergeant LaForge again. "I know you men want to leave early in the morning, so I won't keep you any longer. It's a long jaunt to where you have to go—on foot or horseback. Please stop in and say good-bye before you leave." And with that, it was over. Within a few hours, they would all be going their separate ways. Tom's feelings were mixed. He had just been given a great chance to have what he wanted—his certification as a medical doctor—and would survive army life, he was sure. After almost being hanged and then his adventure to the Bear Paws with Pete, he felt that he could handle almost anything. But he had been thinking about Judith. She would be leaving early in the morning on the train to Chicago, so after he was settled in, he made his way over to see her.

Tom had gotten used to working with Judith and having her around. He thought it only right to be honest with her about what had happened to him in Cantana and his brush with the hangman's noose. He also confessed to her that he really wasn't a doctor. She didn't seem to mind. "I have seen what you can do, Doctor Brumett. I don't know how anyone could do better. You're a bona fide doctor in my eyes," she told him with a sweet smile and a hug.

"Do you think you will like living in Chicago with an aunt and uncle you have never met?" he asked. "What about your desire to accompany the Nez Perce to Washington State?"

"After much contemplation, I figured it was best if I let the Nez Perce return to the main tribe and start out life afresh without me. My presence will only cause questions and confusion. The general gave me the address to the Colville Reservation, so I will keep in touch with Michael that way," Judith answered.

"Do you ever think you might come back to Montana for a visit?" Tom asked shyly, looking at the ground. Judith smiled and reached up to touch his cheek with the back of her hand. "You never can tell, Doctor Brumett. I must see if there is anything for me in Chicago. I suppose my aunt and uncle are my guardians now, and I would want to secure their blessings on anything I do from now on. I will write you, though, if you'd like. I would sure enjoy a letter from you now and then, to hear of the exploits of the young army surgeon I have gotten to know and admire. Now I must go and pack, for the train leaves early from Havre. Will you see me off?"

"I was hoping that you would let me take you to the train station. Maybe we can have tea together before you go," Tom said with a smile.

15
Back to the Medicine Line

Pete and his two companions, Marshal Brenton and Sergeant LaForge, rode north across the bleak, endless springtime prairie with its faded yellow grasses matted down by the weight of winter's snow. The return journey was certainly different than the one he and Tom had taken several months ago. The weather was mild, the breezes soft, and the few nights they had to camp out on the open plain were actually agreeable. Pete missed Tom already, and Arliss the buffalo soldier, who had saved their lives. He wished them both well in his heart and hoped that life would give Chief Michael and his band of Nez Perce, who had been humbled by circumstances beyond their control, a new chance and future.

"There it is," said Marshal Brenton, pointing ahead to an almost indiscernible dark spot on the horizon. It was Cantana. With few landmarks to guide, if a stranger was off by a fraction of a degree either way, he would pass on into Canada and not even know it. But it was home, and they all had someone to come back to. The men were tempted to break into a canter with the horses, but they were tired too, and they must not forget the pack mules, faithfully lumbering on behind them.

It was midday as the three men rode into town, and everything looked the way they had left it. They saw no one on the streets, but that would be a fairly normal day for a town that was buildings rich and population poor.

"Whoa!" Marshal Brenton said, holding up his hand in cavalry fashion. "Let's stop at the livery first and see Bill Hester. I made him acting marshal in our absence, Pete, and he will tell us how things have been faring. And these horses and mules need a good goin' over too." Stepping down and stretching, they called out into the darkness of the livery stable door. "Ho, Bill!" the marshal shouted. Soon, the old blacksmith stuck his head out, peeking around the corner of the door.

"Marshal! Glad to see ya and young Peter. I was beginnin' to get a mite worried," Bill said, wiping the sweat and ash from his face with his faded blue scarf. He put his hammer down next to the hot forge to shake hands with the three men. "This is my day to make nails, you see," he said with a big grin. Bill Hester removed the badge from his chest, and buffing it on his sleeve, handed it to Marshal Brenton.

"No, you keep that, Bill. I want you to stay sworn in as my deputy—it's a powerful comfort knowing I can count on you." Bill Hester blushed and nodded his head, obviously touched by the marshal's statement. "How's things in town, Bill? Any trouble?"

"No, pretty quiet. I did have a visit from some young Mountie, though, lookin' for the sergeant here. I sent him over to Melinda. Didn't say what he wanted."

David glanced over at Jim LaForge. "See you later, Bill. Take care of them horses and mules, will ya? I haven't been home yet." The marshal and the Mountie waved at Pete and Bill Hester and then crossed the street to go home.

"It sounds like they sent someone out to find you, Jim. I hope I didn't get you into trouble."

"I don't think so, Dave. Regina understood that I would be on American soil and considered the risks worthy if I could help bring these men to justice. The truth is that I really didn't expect to return alive. That's why I needed to know that Marta was safe and in the home of my best friends." Brenton embraced his longtime friend around the shoulder. "Enough of that now, Jim. Let's see if we can get some hot food and then maybe a bath."

Pete walked to the marshal's office and opened the door. The room was chilly and dark but familiar. He hadn't been there for many months, but it was still home. Instead of hot coffee and frying bacon, the room reeked of stale coal ashes and kerosene. Leaning his rifle against the wall, he stood in the dark silence for several moments. "This will not do!" he said out loud as he went to each of the lanterns in the room, quickly trimming their wicks with an old pair of shears from his desk and wiping out the soot from their blackened chimneys, lighting them as he went. Soon, a shadowy golden light shone out against the walls and floor as it had before. Then, opening the creaking door of the stove, he cast in several chunks of coal from the box in the corner and drizzled it with kerosene, throwing in a lit match.

"There! That will soon chase out the darkness and chill, and I'll have a pot of coffee boiling as in the old days. Now for a shave and a bath!" He walked to the wooden shelf in the corner which held his shaving cup and razor, his soap, and a bottle of witch hazel. Standing in front of a mirror for the first time in months, he was shocked at the gauntness of his face, revealing that he had lost weight. Pete had not shaved or cut his hair since last November, and he looked like a crazy wild mountain man.

"I think I'll let the barber up the street tend to this. I am a mess!" Pete said out loud. The door opened behind him, and thinking it was the marshal, Pete didn't bother to look up.

"So, you finally decided to come out of hibernation and see us. You look like an old bear!" said a teasing but slightly irritated voice.

"Alice!" Pete exclaimed, turning to face her.

"When were you going to let me know you were home?" she said as she hurried to him.

Pete held her hands in his. "Sorry, Alice, but we just got into town. I wanted to get a bath and a shave and haircut first. I don't smell so good right now."

Alice did not answer but put her arms around Pete's waist and rested her head against his chest. She had missed him terribly—she hadn't even known how much until she saw him again, even in his disheveled state. "I'm sorry too, Peter. I didn't mean to nag. It's been such a long time, and I expected you back sooner. I know that something dreadful must have happened."

"It's been quite an adventure, Alice. If I was smart enough, I would put it all down in a book. But I would like to tell you all about it sometime, if you have a mind to listen."

Alice looked into his eyes and brushed the long hair out of his face. "Go ahead and get spruced up, and then come see me. I will have a good hot supper waiting for you and a fire," she said, kissing him and opening the door to leave. "I want to know everything that has happened."

* * *

Later that afternoon, after a visit to the town barber and a good soaking in his copper tub, Pete found himself once more at the Granfield Hotel seated in the parlor next to Alice. He had forgotten how peaceful it was there, and he consumed a hearty meal of more delicate fare than he had eaten in a long time—roast beef with Yorkshire pudding. As Pete and Alice sat down together on the comfortable leather couch in the parlor before a crackling fire, his weariness began to catch up with him. Fearing that he might drift away in sleep, Pete set his teacup and saucer on the table before him. He cleared his throat and sat up straight.

"Sorry, Alice, for nodding off. It's as if for the first time in many months I am completely at rest."

Alice said nothing, but answered with a smile. She didn't seem to mind, and she held him close. Pete let his eyes close and once more enjoyed the fragrance of the perfume that had long faded from the scarf she had tied around his neck late last autumn.

"Alice?" he said, his eyes still closed. "I thought about you all the time I was gone. I couldn't help it."

"I thought about you too, Peter. I can't imagine what you went through, the hardships and trials. I asked the dear Lord to bring you back safely to me, and He did. I suppose that was a selfish prayer on my part."

Pete opened his eyes. "Tom and I got ourselves into some pretty fixes out on the trail, and several times I thought it might be over for sure, but it was as if Someone was always there, leading us to do the right thing. I called it Providence, but do you suppose that it could have been God?"

Alice's green eyes glistened with moisture. "I know it was, Peter. He loves you so much, more than I could ever do. I wish you would learn to trust Him like I have."

Pete put his arm around Alice's shoulder and was thoughtful. "Chief Michael of the Nez Perce Indians spoke often of the Great Father and His Son Jesus. He seemed to set great store by those two Names, more than just a fondness but a love, like he knew them personally."

Pete was silent for a long time, and Alice thought he might have fallen asleep again until he finally spoke. "Alice, I know you have tried to help me understand about Jesus the Savior, and I've listened only to make you happy. I guess I wasn't foolin' anybody, was I? I would consider it a kindness if you would take that black book there on the table and explain it all to me again."

* * *

Seated around the fire in the parlor of the Brenton's storefront home, David and Melinda and Jim and Marta LaForge were cheerful, sipping their tea and discussing the events of the last several weeks. The mysterious visitor from the North-West Mounted Police had been the LaForge's son, Daniel, who had recently been assigned to his own remote detachment and was on one of his long patrols. As his father had done for years before him, he had stopped by Cantana for a visit and was surprised to find his mother there staying with the Brentons. He was also surprised to learn that his father had gone to the Bear Paws.

Not able to stay long because he had his own duties, he comforted his mother and assured her that "Father" would soon be back—safe and sound. He would try to swing back through on his next patrol.

The subject finally came around to what would be the next chapter in their lives. David and Melinda had for years discussed moving to Oregon country near the ocean and living out their remaining years there. Jim LaForge and Marta were not so sure of their future plans. Jim still had to return to Regina, report on his mission, and settle up his affairs before retirement. He did not look forward to putting his wife through a long, grueling trip on horseback or a lonely, circuitous train ride back to Regina. He had always wanted to explore the United States, but what about his son, Daniel, who had joined the Mounties to follow in his pa's footsteps? If he and Marta spent a lot of time in America, when would they ever see him again?

"Jim, I was thinking. I am soon to hand in my badge, and I know now that Pete is more than able to marshal this town. It's no secret that Melinda and I have made plans to settle in Oregon, and we would like to go before the cold weather sets in again in the fall. About a year and a half ago, while making a visit there to extradite a prisoner back to Cantana, I put money down on a wonderful four-hundred-acre farm I saw there. It's paid off now. It has lots of fruit trees, pastures for cattle, and two nice cottages on it. One of those cottages, along with two hundred acres, is yours, folks, if you will take it. Maybe we're getting ahead of ourselves, but why don't you and Marta come with us? Oregon is beautiful country if you don't mind a little rain, and it's not so far from Canada. We could journey up the coast now and then and take the train to visit Daniel, and he could always come and see us. What do you folks say?"

Jim and Marta LaForge looked at each other and smiled. "This is kind of sudden, Dave. We need to talk it over and let the notion settle in. Can you give us some time to think about it?" Jim squeezing his wife's hand as he spoke, but he knew in his heart what the answer would be.

"Sure, Jim. You and Marta take as long as you like."

16
The People Go Home

Arliss Moore stood beside his horse, surveying the great expanse before him. The sun was shining, but the low clouds in the mountains declared that it wouldn't last as the smell of distant rain and the rumble of thunder was in the air. The bright green grass waved in the warm wind that came rushing in from the distant Pacific Ocean. Arliss watched as the small but proud band of Nez Perce made their way down to the village on the Colville Reservation. A brave had been sent ahead to announce their coming, and soon, a great crowd of people walked out to meet them. Arliss could see many braves with women and children, some on horses but most on foot.

Chief Michael and his beautiful young wife Snowbird led their small group to meet them, and though Michael held his head up high, his heart was filled with apprehension. He was young and had expected to live out his life in the Bear Paw Mountains, always wary of outsiders and always alone, burdened with the responsibilities of being chief. But now, he was to be reunited with his great people, the Nimíipuu, and to perhaps relinquish his authority to another chief and be absorbed into obscurity among them. But this was what he wanted. It was best for the small band of people he had tried to shepherd and who had suffered for so many years.

Among the growing crowd of people below the hill appeared an older man, his face wizened by years of care and sorrow, weathered by the elements but still handsome. He seemed to be greatly venerated, as the people willingly stood aside to let him pass. Perhaps he was a great chief or member of the council—Arliss did not know. As Michael approached, the old man stood still, his back straight and his head held high.

As he came within a few feet of the man, Michael held up his hand, signaling to his followers that they had finally reached their destination. Alone, Michael walked forward, pausing for a brief moment, and then, unable to hold back his tears and emotion, he embraced the old man. The old one kissed him and held him close for a good long while as the two wept together. Raising his right hand to the little band that stood before him, the aged warrior motioned to them that it was acceptable for them to approach, and he embraced them one by one.

As the crowd of people turned to walk back to their final home on the reservation, Chief Michael turned for a moment and glanced up the hill to where Arliss stood.

Holding up his hand to the buffalo soldier who had been his friend, he sent his silent word of gratitude that he was now content. Arliss knew in his heart that this would probably be the last time he would see his friends—a great people humbled against their will. He quickly mounted his horse and turned to leave.

Now where do I go from here? he questioned within himself, realizing for the first time that he was again alone and without a purpose. He had been so concerned with training the Nez Perce and seeing them to Colville that he had not thought of what would come after. His temporary reinstatement in the army as a first sergeant ended with the completion of his mission here. He could accept the general's offer and return to Fort Assiniboine, but that was forever a part of his past. There was always his home up in the Bear Paw Mountains, but somehow that place had become distasteful and lonely to him. He still had family in Texas, but he quickly remembered why he had left. Where could he go where he would be treated like a man and judged by his merit and character, and not by what men saw on the outside? Did such a place exist?

"I will find out!" he muttered under his breath, and giving his horse a gentle nudge with his heels, he set out on a path for Cantana.

The End

"Let me be a free man, free to travel, free to stop, free to work, free to trade where I choose, free to choose my own teachers, free to follow the religion of my fathers, free to talk, think and act for myself— and I will obey every law or submit to the penalty."

Chief Joseph

www.ingramcontent.com/pod-product-compliance
Lightning Source LLC
Chambersburg PA
CBHW071237250626
47163CB00001B/212